ANGEL OF VENGEANCE

ANGEL OF VENGEANCE

TREVOR O. MUNSON

TITAN BOOKS

ANGEL OF VENGEANCE
ISBN: 9781848568556

Published by
Titan Books
A division of Titan Publishing Group Ltd.
144 Southwark St.
London SE1 0UP

First edition: February 2011
10 9 8 7 6 5 4 3 2 1

Did you enjoy this book? We love to hear from our readers.
Please e-mail us at: **readerfeedback@titanemail.com**
or write to Reader Feedback at the above address.

To receive advance information, news, competitions, and exclusive
offers online, please sign up for the Titan newsletter on our website:
www.titanbooks.com

A CIP catalogue record for this title is available from the British Library.

Printed and bound in the United States of America.

To my parents, Tom and Sharon,
whose love and encouragement has always served as the
light that allowed me to chase my dreams to whatever
dark places they might lead.

PROLOGUE

Black doctor's satchel clutched tight, I stop beneath the naked bulb that burns next to a chipped paint door marked 3B. It's late for a house call, but then I'm no doctor.

Knock-knock. I wait.

3B swings open and a scrawny white guy blinks out at me. With his oversized Adam's apple, thinning blond hair, and wire-framed glasses, he looks like a mild-mannered accountant. He smiles at me friendly-like. It's a sweet smile. A smile you can trust. But if there's one thing I've learned over the years, it's that looks can be deceiving. I should know.

"Michael Ensinger?" I ask, and watch as a look of suspicion creeps across his bland features.

"Who's askin'?"

"My friend here," I say, showing him the pearl-handled .38 revolver I've taken from the satchel.

"Woah, hey. Hey," Michael says. I enjoy seeing the sullen look depart as he puts his soft, never-seen-a-hard-day's-work-in-his-whole-life hands up in front of him like a bank teller in an old western. "What is this? What's goin' on?"

"We need to talk."

"'Kay. S'talk."

"Not here. Inside. Can I come in?"

Scared, he nods nervous consent.

"No. You have to say it. Can I come in?"

With only eyes for my gun, he says, "Yeah, yeah. Come in."

Green light. I back him inside at gunpoint. I close the door behind me, spin the bolt lock, look around. The place is run down, but neatly kept, everything in its place.

Behind him on the tube, a bound-and-gagged naked blonde is being dragged across a room by her hair by a guy in a black hood. Looks like I interrupted Mikey in the middle of a little sadistic jack-off session.

"Nice show. Find it on PBS?"

"Screw you, man. What d'you want with me?"

My lack of response makes him more nervous and he swallows. I watch that huge Adam's apple bob up and down inside his Ichabod Crane-neck. Best not stare too long.

"A-are you okay?" He has seen something he doesn't like in my dark crystal-ball eyes. Something that doesn't bode well for a long, healthy future.

"I'm fine. Where's your bathroom?"

He gestures vaguely. "D-down the hall."

"Let's go."

"What? Why? I mean, I thought you just wanted to talk."

"I do. In the bathroom."

Ensinger looks like he wants to argue the point, so I cock the gun. It dummies him up nice and I follow him down the short hall and into the ugly tile bathroom. I pull the door shut behind us and inspect the facilities. The tub is filthy. It will have to be cleaned.

Keeping the gun on him, I root under the bathroom sink and come up with a scrub brush and a can of Comet. I hold them out.

"Clean the tub. It's disgusting."

He looks at me like I must be joking, gives me a smart-ass smile. "So what, you go around breaking into places and force people to clean?"

I smack the grin right off his face. His glasses go flying. He crumples by the tub. It's all the answer he gets. "Get to it."

Cowering, he fumbles for his glasses, puts them back on. Then, with jittering hands, he runs the hot water, sprinkles the Comet and begins to scrub like a good boy.

Behind him I carefully remove my tailored suit jacket and roll up my sleeves. Noticing my increasing state of undress from the corner of his eye, Ensinger stops and looks at me nervously. I point to the tub. "Focus." He goes back to it. The rhythmic scrape of the brush against the porcelain sounds like a train locomotive picking up speed for a long uphill haul. Seems appropriate.

"What's going on? I don't know what's going on," he says, sounding like a scared nine year-old boy.

"What's going on—" I explain as I remove my fedora and set it beside the sink where it will be safe and out of the way, "is

11

I've come to see you on behalf of someone you know real well."

"Who?"

"Elizabeth Lowery."

His eyes go wide at the mention of the name. The brush stops. He turns and looks at me. "N-no. I didn't—That wasn't me. The—the cops, they had the wrong guy. That's why they let me go. They had the wrong guy."

"Uh-uh. They had the right guy. They only let you go because Elizabeth was too scared of you to testify. Isn't that right?"

"No."

"Way I heard it, when you were done with her, the docs had to sew up parts that shouldn't have to be sewn up."

"No. You got it wrong. I swear to God you got it wrong."

"You're not working," I say. I set the gun down—I don't really need it, it's more for effect than anything else—and light a smoke.

Nearly done now, he goes back to it, scrubbing away as he tries to work it all out.

"So what, she—she hired you to come here?"

"No. I've never met her. This was my idea. Call it a hobby," I say, doing my best impression of a smokestack.

"I'm sorry. I'm sorry. I shouldn't have done it. It was wrong and—and I'm sorry," he mewls.

"It's okay. I understand."

"Y-you do?"

"Sure. You like to hurt girls. I used to know someone like you. He liked to hurt women too. Only difference was he was my old man and the woman he liked to hurt was my mother.

He beat her to death and went to jail while I was still too young to stop him… " I shake my head, blow smoke. "Regret like that, it stays with ya."

The scrubbing stops again. Beside the tub, Ensinger turns and looks at me as I loosen the knot in my tie, take it off. "Of course, now, my mom, she chose him. Elizabeth Lowery didn't even get that chance, did she? She never got to make the decision one way or the other because she didn't know you existed. And if she had, she wouldn't have given you the time of day, would she, Mikey? That's what really gets you, isn't it? That's why you pick the ones you pick."

Ensinger just stares at me, the truth of things frozen on his face.

"Rinse it," I say.

I extinguish the butt in the drip from the sink faucet and drop it into a ziplock bag I keep among the other items—glass vials, funnel, ball-gag, hacksaw—in the satchel.

Hands trembling, Ensinger spins the knobs and turns the showerhead on, rinsing the frothy gray bubbles down the drain. Finished, he sits with his back against the tub and looks up at me.

"Nice job." I pick up the gun and gesture with it. "Get in."

"Please—please don't hurt me."

"I don't like to repeat myself. It makes me sore. Real sore, if you want to know the truth. Get in the tub."

He sees in my eyes that there's no room for argument. He gets up and gets in.

"Lock the drain."

With a sob, he pulls the metal drain tab up, and looks up at me with the same feverish, glassy-eyed stare I imagine a cow must give the butcher just before the stropped blade is dragged across its neck.

"I'll never do it again. I swear to God I'll never do it again."

I let go now. I'm over the brink. The change has begun and just as with the moment of release during orgasm, Moses himself couldn't hold it back. The pain of transformation is as awful as it is sweet. Bone is displaced as my brow wrenches forward. My face elongates. My fangs grow. My jaw comes unhinged. My eyes grow black as they fill with blood.

Seeing it happen, the look in Michael's eyes tells me he's just now realizing how much more there was to learn about the reality he thought he knew. I don't feel the least bit bad for him. Predators like him are a waste of skin in my book, which is why I only hunt predators like him. No women. No children. No innocents. Those are the rules. I'm no hero, but the way I figure it, if I've got to kill people—and I do—might as well be ones who deserve killin'. It's how I live with myself, so to speak. It's how I deal with what I've become.

"I know you won't," I say.

1

Nightfall comes with an ache. I feel the sinking sun deep in my bones the way old people sense a coming storm. My thirst awakens like the first signs of narcotic withdrawal. Parched with a sandy desert thirst, I rise.

I push open the lid of the industrial-size deep freeze that serves as my coffin. The freezer preserves me; slows the cancerous rot that gnaws me from the inside out during my waking hours. Though vastly slower than normal decomposition, the ever-constant stink of decay is an ugly truth about being undead. One of those little tidbits no one tells you about before you become a vampire.

Frostbitten air trails me like a cape as I step naked into the dark confines of my North Hollywood digs. The place isn't much to look at, just a shabby two-bit office with a kitchenette and half-bath, but it's home.

I don't have much in the way of furniture or appliances; I'm not what you'd call an acquirer. I can list all my major possessions in twenty-five words or less: desk, chairs, answering machine, phone, filing cabinet, mini-fridge, freezer, fedora, five suits, two pairs of shoes, a car. Oh yeah, and a gun. The adjectives'll cost ya extra.

I move out of the kitchenette into the office proper. The freezer motor hums dully in tune with distant traffic noise from the 101. There is a numb, mildly pleasant pain as my frozen limbs begin to thaw. I barely notice. I have bigger concerns. Shivering, not with cold but with thirst, I stiff-leg it over to my desk and twist the light on. I punch a button on my answering machine. No messages while I was on ice. No nothing.

My trembling fingers tug a side drawer open and fumble with the zipper of my worn leather kit. In the light, I notice that they are coated with a fine layer of dust from the graveyard dirt that pads the bottom of my cold-storage coffin.

Time to fix.

I go to the small refrigerator that sits on the floor just below the office's single aluminum foil-covered window. The neighbors probably think I'm running a meth lab, but the fact of the matter is the sun and I aren't exactly on what you'd call speaking terms. Haven't been for a while now.

I kneel. My frozen knee joints pop with the force of a twenty-two caliber pistol. I open the refrigerator door to find only five crimson glass vials remain. Damn. I thought there were more. I grab one and hold it up to the refrigerator light, enjoying the brownish-red tint of the liquid that hugs the vial walls. Except for red, vampires see the world in only black and white. So all things red are to be savored. Adored.

Eager for my fix, I hurry now. I carry the vial back to the desk. I take an old-fashioned, sawbones-style needle from the sterilizer and assemble it, screwing the tip and casing together. I pop the cap from the vial and poke the gleaming tip into the ichor. I pull the plunger back, drawing a good portion of the thick blood into the casing, before carefully replacing the cap on the vial, saving the remainder for later. Then I strangle one ice-cold bicep with a rubber garrote, pulling it tight with sharpened teeth.

Over the years, mainlining has evolved as my favorite way of taking blood. There is a comfort in the ritual that I have grown to love. A holdover from my days as a smack addict. Any junkie will tell you that the effects are stronger and the relief more immediate and a little goes a lot longer when you shoot it. What can I say? Old habits die hard.

I smack my arm, searching for a non-recessed vein. Finding one, I jam the needle home before it can slip away on me like a snake in water. I have to jam it hard to break through my permafrost skin. I depress the plunger. Goddamn but it feels good. Even old blood. Fresh is best, but any blood will do. Just so long as it's human.

I withdraw the needle, lick the tip clean. Tasty. My jangling nerves recede with my teeth. My thirst abates.

As always, the initial high makes me sleepy. I drowse in my chair, staring from under half pound lids at the framed black-and-white photograph perched on one corner of my desk. It's a snapshot of me posing with my old band mates, taken after a show at the Million Dollar Theater on Third and Broadway in late '43. Good guys all of them. And me the only white boy in the bunch.

I reach out with sandbag arms and take the frame in both hands for a better look at the me I used to be. Tall and too thin; almost sickly. Probably from the drugs. Dark hair. Darker eyes. Wise-guy grin. A chin in constant need of a shave. Good looking but not too good looking, if you know what I mean.

I shake my head. I barely recognize that kid. With all I've seen and all I've done, I feel I must look different, but I probably don't. Hard to know for sure.

Despite rumors to the contrary, vampires do have reflections. The random observer would see my human image in a mirror, but when I look I can only see the monster inside; the way I look when I transform. When every day's a bad day in the mirror, eventually you just stop looking.

The black phone in front of me rings shrilly. Enough nostalgia. I set the photo down and pick up.

"Yeah?"

A smoky female voice blows over the line. "Mr. Angel?"

"Speaking."

"My name's Reesa Van Cleef. I have a job I'd like to discuss with you."

"What's that?"

"I'd rather talk about it in person. Would it be possible to meet?"

"Anything's possible. When's good?"

"I'm free tomorrow during the day. I could come by your office—"

"No good. I'm busy tomorrow."

"The next day then."

"Actually, Ms. Van Cleef, I prefer to work at night. I'm a little funny like that. Call it a quirk."

"Oh, I see…"

"Something wrong?"

"No, it's just that—well, I work nights too. I'm a performer; a burlesque dancer. I do a retro lounge act at the Tropicana five nights a week."

"I see."

"Would it be too much trouble to ask you to come to me?"

Normally it would. Normally if a client wanted my help they could damn well come here. But seeing as I could use the work and being as this particular client was a burlesque dancer, well, I figured I could make an exception just this once.

"Sure. When?"

"How 'bout tonight? My first performance is at ten. It's a little racy, but if you're not the type whose sensibilities are easily offended why don't you come see it? We can grab a drink at the bar between shows."

"Sure," I say again. It's a long time since I've been out on the town for anything other than work or blood.

"Great. I'll put your name on the list," she says in a voice as playful as a tongue on an earlobe. "You'll know me. I'll be the one in the red feather boa and not much else."

"I'll be the one in the fedora."

2

I pull my vintage, blood red Mercedes-Benz 300 SL Roadster into a metered slot just up the street from the Tropicana. I bought her new back in '57 and it's a love affair that has stood the test of time. Ain't love grand?

I'm early so I take my kit out and go through the familiar process of fixing. I assemble the needle, tie off my arm, draw the blood. Because my skin is almost translucent in its alabaster whiteness I rarely have trouble finding a vein. Even the recessed ones. I slip the tip in, depress the plunger and... everything's Jake.

Settling back into the Benz's loving embrace, I let myself drowse in my euphoric state for a few minutes, enjoying my high. Lids at half-mast, I watch the red taillights of cars as they motor past on Melrose. When I slowly rise to full awareness fifteen minutes later I see it's ten-o-five. Now I'm late. Swell. I shake my head to clear it, get out, head back up the street to the club.

I move past the long losers' line at the door and walk right up to a pony-tailed doorman with a chest like a beer keg. I tell him I'm on the list. Turns out I am. He unhooks a purple velvet cordon and lets me in.

The small dark forties-style lounge smells of beer and cigarettes and betrayal and sex. Old pick-up lies hang faintly in the air. The joint hasn't changed a bit, which I take to mean the owners are either visionary about the cyclical nature of trends or just cheap. Maybe both. Small, intimate candlelit tables punctuate the room. On one side, a small thrust stage takes up the entire west wall. Big bare glowing light bulbs stand like soldiers at attention along the perimeter of the stage, as if protecting the six-piece swing band from the riff-raff. Aside from me, the members of the band are the only ones in the place dressed the part.

I look around for the bar. I find it set back into the wall opposite the stage. The band plays me over the shoe-worn carpet to a tall stool. I order a Scotch on the rocks from a bartender with a thin moustache and watery eyes that remind me of two black pearls sunk deep in oysters. Judging from the gin-blossoms in his cheeks, slinging drinks isn't the job for him. Kind of like a pill-head working the counter at a pharmacy. But that's his problem, not mine.

I swivel around on the stool, eyeing the people that take up the seats at the tables scattered about. Reesa draws an eclectic crowd. Mostly gay couples of both sexes, but thrown in among them are tie-loosened Hollywood types, horny college students, and a few leering Persians.

All eyes are directed at the stage where the white-tuxedoed bandleader tempos the Cole Porter down and takes to the mike to introduce the delightful, delicious, de-lovely Reesa Van Cleef. Cheers, applause, whistles, and hoots follow the introduction, growing in volume and intensity as the lady herself, veiled behind a wall of red feathers, takes center stage.

She's gorgeous; stunning in that golden era Hollywood screen siren way, when women carried an alluring air of mystery about them. When they all seemed to know something you didn't, and found the fact amusing. She might have walked right out of a frame of an old black-and-white Bogart flick. The only tip-off that she is not a product of my own bygone day is the fact that her hair, which she wears in a forties-style forward-curled pompadour, is brilliant Kool-Aid red. My favorite color. I'm not much for smiling, but I smile now. I didn't think they were making them like her anymore. Glad to see I was wrong.

Somewhere a bubble machine works its magic. The band dusts off an old tromboney ditty and Reesa glides into motion. Her bright eyes flirt as she teases the crowd, giving us titillating peek-a-boos of her moon-pale skin, racetrack curves, and full Jane Russell bosoms with small rosebud-pink nipples. Call me old-fashioned, but this is what a strip show should be. The term striptease suggests nudity with a sense of fun and playfulness. There's none of that in the way the strippers of today ply their trade. It's all just gyrating, g-string-in-your-face, mercenary flesh for hire. Ugly. A show like that leaves you feeling low, like you're lesser for it, like you've been conned. Not that I don't ever go. I do. Joints like that are open late and I'm a late-night kind of guy. But watching Reesa do her red-feather shimmy reminds me of something I've almost forgotten. It's as if her seductive movements are capable of weaving a spell and casting me back in time. I feel transported. I feel like a kid again.

I feel alive.

The show goes by faster than summer vacation. When it's over I blink and look around feeling like I've come out of a trance. My highball of McAllen, which was delivered unbeknownst to me, sits melted and untouched at my elbow. I shake my head to clear it. I need to get a hold on myself. I'm here on business. It won't do to come across like some drooling schoolboy.

To have something to do, I shake out a butt, light it. The bartender is instantly on the spot to play the ever-popular game of fuck with the smoker.

"Sorry, you'll have to put that out, sir. There's no smoking allowed in the Tropicana," he says.

He doesn't sound too sorry. In fact, he sounds like he enjoys spoiling my good time. I lock eyes with him, my hypnotic stare as impossible to resist as a *Star Trek* tractor beam, and tell him, "I'm not smoking."

A glazed cow-dumb stare comes over his ruddy face. "You're not smoking," he repeats.

"That's right. Now you're going to give me an empty rocks glass to use as an ashtray."

He nods, says nothing, just does it.

"Now you're going to leave me alone until I call you."

"I'm going to leave you alone," he murmurs.

Being undead has a lot of drawbacks, but it's got its advantages too. The hypnotic gaze is one of them.

Grinning, I blow a cloud of secondhand smoke in the guy's face as he goes to stand over by the cash register, which seems to serve the additional purpose of propping him up.

Intermission. The lights come up. Patrons—fags and dykes and Persians alike—file out. I smoke, trying to ignore the butterflies that flop like dying fish in my stomach as I await Reesa's company. I reassure myself that she's probably not half as attractive up close. Can't be. I only ever met one other dame who was. This was all just a trick of the distance, the makeup, the lights. Up close I'll see the flaws; the chinks in her Venus di Milo complexion; the cracks running through her Mona Lisa smile.

I check my watch and toss back my drink and signal for another, a double. Why the hell not? I can't get drunk unless the alcohol has already been absorbed into a victim's blood, and besides it gives me a prop; something to do with my hands. I mash my smoke out, light another.

"How do you do it?"

I swivel around to find her standing there in a red silk kimono embroidered with dragons. Immediately I realize I couldn't have been more wrong about her looks. She's the real deal; every bit as lovely up close as she appeared on stage. Lovelier. I feel a strange disappointment. A noticeable flaw would have been a welcome thing; would have put me back in control of myself.

"What's that?" I ask, glad at least that I don't sound like a nervous schoolboy. It's about eighty years too goddamn late for that.

"Get away with smoking. I can't believe no one's said anything to you yet. Usually they're real pricks about it. Won't even let me do it in my own dressing room."

"Yeah, well, we came to an agreement. Would you like one?" I say, picking up the pack and shaking one out.

Reesa hesitates a moment, but finally takes it, game if I am. Red manicured nails carry the butt up to a mouth like a Christmas bow. I've never felt jealous of a cigarette before. Guess there really is a first time for everything. She waits for me to light it. Her wish is my command.

"I hope you're Mick Angel," she says, drawing in a lungful. "Otherwise I'm gonna feel real silly."

"That's me," I say. "Can I buy you a drink?"

"I drink free here, but you can order me one." There is a whisper of silk on vinyl as she slides onto the stool next to me. Now I'm jealous of the stool.

"All right. Let me guess—you look like a martini kinda gal."

"Good guess. And I bet you're having Scotch."

We smile. Kindred spirits.

"Vodka?" I ask, hoping it's not.

She shakes her head, electric-red curls bouncing around that lovely face. "Gin. Three olives. Dirty."

"Dirty huh?"

"The dirtier the better."

I call the bartender over and order her drink. He notices Reesa smoking and starts to put the kibosh on it, but I cut him short, telling him he's got it all wrong again. This time a flicker of doubt crosses his face. That's the problem with the hypnotic gaze. It's a nice tool to have, but some people are more receptive to it than others. It usually correlates with intelligence. I wonder if I've already over-used it with this fella, and if the situation is about to become awkward, but then the troubled look in his eyes disappears and he goes to mix the drink.

"So, you've been here before?" she asks.

I nod. "But it's been a while."

"Ever catch my show?" she asks.

I shake my head. "I don't think you were doing the show last time I was here, but I'd've been back sooner if I'd known what I was missing out on."

She likes this. It earns me a smile.

"This seems like your kind of place."

"Yeah?"

It's her turn to nod. "I mean, this place is old school and you seem like an old school kinda guy."

I smile wryly. "Old school. That's me all right." Emphasis on the old.

"I like old school," Reesa assures me. "It's a compliment."

"Then that's how I'll take it."

We smile. The drinks come. I enjoy seeing the perfect imprint her full bottom lip leaves on the rim of her martini glass.

As much as I'd like to make this about pleasure, it's about business, so I get to the point and ask her how I can help her.

"I want you to find my fourteen year-old sister, Raya. She's gone missing."

"How long?"

"A couple months now. She was living with me and my boyfriend, but she ran away."

I smell a lie in there somewhere, but I let it go. Everybody lies. I'm more disturbed by the fact that she has a boyfriend, if you want to know the truth.

"And no one's looking for her?"

"The cops say they're looking, but they haven't found her. What's one more teenage runaway to them?"

"Why was she living with you instead of your parents?"

"If you knew my family you wouldn't have to ask. Let's just say my dad put the fun in dysfunction and let it go at that."

I nod. "So she was living with you and your boyfriend?"

"Ex-boyfriend. I left him a week or two later."

Hearing it does my heart good. "Mind if I ask why?" I'm prying. So sue me.

"You want the short list or the long?"

"Just gimme the highlights."

"Well, on top of being a complete shitbag of a human being, it turns out he was fucking everything he could get that little pecker of his into."

"I see."

"I'm sorry. I shouldn't talk like that. It's not ladylike."

"No one would ever mistake you for anything but a lady," I say, cashing in on another smile.

"Anyway, it's my own fault. I broke my rule about never dating anyone with anything to do with Hollywood. I know better. Of course the icing on the shit cake was his endearing meth addiction."

"He was a tweaker, huh?"

Reesa nods, absently pulling a red curl out and letting it spring back into place as she speaks. "We both were. That's part of why I left. I was sick of it. I hated living that way. I wanted to clean myself up. So I left. Went into rehab. When I got out six weeks later I tried to find my sister, but… " She shrugs helplessly, shakes her head.

"No dice," I finish for her.

She shakes her head again. "So, do you think you can help me, Mr. Angel?" Holding her martini glass in both hands, Reesa drinks, watching me with big gorgeous doe-eyes as she does it.

"I could, but I'll be honest, I don't come cheap. I charge five hundred a day plus expenses."

"Money I've got. A girl can make a pretty good living taking her clothes off, or hadn't you heard?"

I match her smirk for smirk and take my notepad out and flip it open to a blank page. "Have you talked to your ex since you left?"

"Do you call the warden after you break out of prison?"

"Good point. But I should talk to him. Your sister lived there with you. Maybe she forgot something when she left and went back for it. Maybe she's tried to call and get in touch with you. Anyway, it's a place to start. What's his name and number?"

Reluctantly she gives them to me. I chicken-scratch the name Vin Prince and two numbers in my pad—one for a cell, the other for his production company. "Address?"

"I don't know," she tells me. "We lived in Los Feliz when we were together, but last I heard he'd moved to some fancy-schmancy place up in the Hills I'm sure he can't afford."

"I'll find it," I say. Then I ask for the names and numbers of anyone else who might know something about where I can find Raya, along with the addresses of places she frequented. Reesa's embarrassed at how little she can come up with, proving once and for all that the best parenting doesn't get done on crystal meth. In the end I've got the name of an eighteen year-old boyfriend of Raya's and the name of a Hollywood Goth club they went to together, and that's all I've got. It'll have to do.

The last thing I ask for is a picture of Raya; something I can show around. Reesa says she thinks she has one in her dressing room and goes to get it. I watch her go. I'm reminded of the ocean. I light a cigarette. I wait.

When she comes back she hands me a snapshot of an attractive fourteen year-old girl with dyed black punk-cut hair caught in the act of rolling her eyes at the camera. The resemblance to Reesa is undeniable. I pocket it.

Though I want to linger, my own addiction is tightening the leash, so I tell Reesa I will look into it, drain my drink, and stand to go.

"Don't you want some money up front?" she asks, batting her lashes at me playful-like. "I thought that's how it worked."

She reaches inside her robe and takes a stash of hundreds from somewhere I don't dare think too long about, being as I'm standing up and all.

"Will a thousand do to start?" I want to tell her to put it

away, to keep it 'til I get some results. That would be the classy thing to do. But I don't. I take it. I take it and hide it in my pocket like something shameful. "It'll do."

"Aren'tcha gonna count it?"

"I trust you," I say.

"But you don't even know me."

"I don't have to. I know where to find you."

One last smile. One last look. I try to acid burn the image of her into my memory. I want to be able to remember her exactly when I fantasize about being that barstool later. I turn and retrace my steps to the door, a cigarette smoke snail-trail the only evidence I came and went.

3

I go back to the car. I fix. I fire up the engine. I drive. Every store, every street that flashes past holds a memory for me of an earlier day, and as always, I find myself reconciling the landmarks of the ghost-of-L.A.-past with that of the present. The dry-ice inland fog that's come smoking in from the Pacific makes the town look all the more spectral.

I hang a right at Fairfax and head south. In the rearview, a set of constant headlights begins to make me wonder if maybe I'm being tailed. Feeling a nervous tightness form in my chest, I take the next left just to see. The headlights, which belong to an older-model Ford pickup, blow past without so much as a hiccup. My chest loosens. I shake my head and fire up a smoke. Maybe I'm getting paranoid in my old age, but if there's one thing I've learned over the years in this business it's that paranoia pays.

I U-turn and continue down Fairfax and pull into the small lot behind the big Canter's Delicatessen sign. I used to love

Canter's back when I could still digest solid food. I would go and eat there after shows way back in the thirties when the deli was still located over in Boyle Heights. I got the pastrami sandwich every time. I liked theirs because it was so lean and rare. I guess I liked things bloody even then.

I get out. I go in, not in search of a pastrami sandwich, but a pay phone. It's bright and busy at this hour. The smell of greasy cooked food washes over me, making my delicate stomach roll uneasily. I swallow hard and make my way over to the phone. Times like this make me rethink my stubborn refusal to adopt a cellular.

I flip my notepad open, drop some change in the slot, and punch up Vin Prince's number. His assistant, a perky skirt by the name of Barbara, picks up. I give a fake name, something Jewish-sounding, and ask to talk with the boss-man, but she tells me he's incommunicado all night. I act all pissed off, telling Babs her boss and me were supposed to get together for drinks to discuss a picture I wrote. I tell her that I'm at the restaurant, that I don't like being stood up, and that if this is how Prince deals with writers I'll just take my script to the next production house down the block because the goddamn town's full of them. Babs gets all flustered-like and explains that Mr. Prince probably just forgot because of some big shindig he's throwing up at his house in the Hills tonight. I ask the address and she tells me before she can think the better of it. Then she asks my name again and I hang up because I can't remember what I told her. Doesn't matter. I found out what I wanted to know. These days this sort of thing is called social engineering.

In my day we just called it bullshitting.

I scratch the address down in my pad, cradle the phone, and exit Canter's, leaving the smell of greasy food and my queasiness behind.

Fancy-schmancy is right. Prince's house is a sight to behold. From a parking spot thirty yards up the winding street at the top of Beachwood Canyon I smoke and take in the splendor of the vintage 1920s home. Nestled in under an oak tree canopy, the expansive Spanish tile roof rests on the tired shoulders of two-story bone-white stucco walls. I can tell at first glance it's too good for a Hollywood asshole like Prince. How do I know he's an asshole? Simple. He works in Hollywood.

From my vantage point I watch as a stream of waxed and gleaming Lexus, Limos, Benz, and Beamers pull up to the wrought-iron gate that surrounds the compound. Leaning out of their windows, evening-attired guests flash gilded invites at the guard who in turn presses a button, causing the automatic gate to Frankenstein-lurch open. Once in, the guests pull around the circular flagstone drive, which has been movie-lit to show their luxury automobiles off to best advantage. There, red-vested valets open their doors, and the guests spill out, moving like royalty along the ridiculous red carpet that runs like a tongue from the mouth of the house. Looks like I won't be getting in that-a-way. Sure, I could drive up and parlor trick my way in, but I can't stand the idea of letting those valets put their grubby paws on my gal. She deserves better. I'll have to look for a back entrance.

I make a firefly of my cigarette butt, exit the Roadster, and start along the twist of road back toward the house. When I reach the property, I duck into the California scrub along its perimeter. Set into the side of a steep Hollywood hill, the long rocky slope is slick as ball bearings on black ice beneath my patent leather shoe soles. I have to use the rough metal rungs of the ten-foot high fence just to keep from bobsledding down on my ass.

A deeper fog sleeps curled in the ravine at the base of the property. Through spaced wrought-iron bars and carefully landscaped foliage, I look back up graded hills to see partygoers mingling atop two large redwood decks that hang off the back of the house and around the illuminated pool and spa below. Jazz music dances in the waterlogged night air. It comes from the gazebo set to one side of the pool. Maybe I have misjudged the host. No one who appreciates jazz enough to hire a band can be all bad. I decide to go in and find out firsthand.

Times like this it would be nice if the stories about vampires being able to turn themselves into bats or mist were true. It would certainly make getting in and out of places a whole lot easier. It's all crap though. At least so far as I know. No one gives you an instruction manual when you get turned. But if that sort of thing is possible, I sure as hell don't know how to go about it.

On the other hand, it is true that vampires are exceedingly strong, a fact I think is only partially due to enhanced supernatural strength. From my experience, all of a vampire's senses are greatly heightened, except for one—touch. Dead, bloodless limbs simply cannot experience the same sensitivity to pressure. The result is a disquieting full-body numbness. On the bright side, less nerve endings mean a much higher pain threshold. Where living flesh would give up under the influence of severe pain, dead flesh won't. The less pain you feel, the more you are capable of enduring. The more you can endure, the stronger you are. So there you go.

I decide to get by on brawn. I grab hold of two wrought-iron rungs and pull. One breaks. The other bends. It's enough. I squeeze my gaunt frame through the gap, careful not to snag my best suit. Feeling tired and dizzy at the expended effort, I brush off and climb the tiered green banks of grass to join the party.

I step through coved French doors into a set-decorated room of another era. A better era. My era. Across the room, over the talking heads of the guests who mingle in the dramatic step-down living room, I see a turreted entryway and a spiral staircase leading up. Expensive prints—they can't be originals—cover the walls. Most of the furniture has been moved out of the living room, but I step down into it to get a better look at a tile fireplace with an interesting Mayan motif which is tucked back into one wall. My head swims. The Tropicana, Reesa, Canter's, and now this place. Everywhere I go tonight, I seem to find myself hunting ghosts.

Oblivious to the magic of the place, and the lesser for it, guests mingle and drink under the high barrel ceiling. So far as I can tell, they are a bland gumbo of Hollywood screenwriters, directors, producers, executives and semi-recognizable actors, each of them believing themselves vastly more interesting than they actually are by virtue of working in the movie biz. I shake my head. This is California. Where's a good earthquake or mudslide when you really need one?

I snare a flute of champagne from the tray of a passing cocktail waitress. Sipping it, I walk up to an aging, Botoxed actress who stands gazing sadly out of a nearby picture window on the distant city lights. I only recognize her because she happens to be the daughter of an actress I used to have a bit of a thing for. Her face poisoned into a death's-head grin, I smile, hoping my eyes don't reflect the horror I feel. She smiles back, but then she doesn't really have a choice.

"Loved your last movie," I lie, not because I didn't love it, but because I didn't see it. Though I'm sure I would have hated it if given the chance.

"Oh thank you, that's so nice of you to say." She takes my hand. We shake. "I still can't understand why it went straight to video."

"Well there's no accounting for taste in this town."

"True."

If possible, she smiles wider. Okay, enough bullshit. I decide to get to the point before she decides she wants to jump the bones of her last fan on the planet.

"Have you seen our host around anywhere?" I ask, this being my clever way of getting Vin Prince, who I've never seen, pointed out to me. I'm good like that.

"Oh yes, I just saw him. Let's see," she turns and looks over at the makeshift bar that has been set up on the ornate tile near the front door. "There he is at the bar."

I look along the curve of her French-manicured nail to see a guy in a tailored Armani suit hand a drink to a fake-boobed blonde twenty years his junior. I dislike him on sight, and not just because his tan is much too dark for the time of year and he wears sunglasses despite being indoors at night. He does his best to hide it, but I know his type immediately. All the money in the world can't scrub slime off a slug. It takes salt to do that.

"I should probably go say hi," I tell the succubus. "Pleasure talking to you."

"You too," she says, trying to be demure, trying to be her mother. "Why don't you come find me later so we can... get better acquainted."

"I'll do that," I lie.

She smiles as I walk away, but then she doesn't really have a choice.

I obstacle course my way across the sunken living room, up the step, and over to the bar where Vin is busy eye-fucking the blonde behind his shades. As I move up behind him I see he stands an inch or two taller than my own six feet. I put my best shit-eater on and clap him on the back a little too hard.

"Vinnie, my man, how's tricks?" I say. I pegged him for the kind of guy who dislikes having his name man-handled and when he turns around I see from his face I was right.

"Vin. The name's *Vin*."

"Oh yeah, sure, right."

Vin slides the shades down his beak so as to get a better look at me. "I know you?"

"Sure you do. I'm at your party, aren't I?"

"That don't mean I know you. That don't mean shit," he says, and pushes his shades back up, hiding his eyes from my hypnotic gaze. For some reason the trick won't work through sunglasses. Sometimes even regular glasses or contacts screw with the works. Go figure.

"You know me," I assure him. "We go way back."

"Wait. Are you a writer?"

"Huh?"

"A writer. A screenwriter I was supposed to meet or some shit like that?"

"Oh, you heard about that?"

"Heard about it? My goddamn assistant called half-shitting-her-panties-scared some homicidal screenwriter she gave my address to was on his way here to put his fountain pen in my eye. Wazzat you?"

"Well, yeah, but I think maybe she got the wrong impression. I'm not a writer. I'm a P.I."

"A what?"

"A private investigator. I've been hired to find Raya Van Cleef. I was hoping maybe you'd give me a few minutes of your time to tell me what you know."

"I don't know shit. How's that? It's just like I told the fuckin' cops—she was here, then she left, and I ain't talked to her since. There. Conversation over. Now hows-about you get outa my fuckin' house, seein' as you wasn't invited in the first fuckin' place?"

The smell of his lie fills my nose. "Be happy to. Right after you answer a couple of questions for me."

Vin's grin is an ugly thing to behold. "Here, walk with me over here a sec," he says to me.

Turning to the blonde, who looks like her brain automatically goes into screen-saver mode when no one's punching her keys, he says, "We'll be right back, baby. You stay here."

The blonde nods obediently and my new pal throws a knotty arm around my shoulder and guides me over to a more private location under a lighted Dali print.

"All right, I'm gonna give it to you straight, just so's we're real clear," he tells me.

"Oh good. I'd like that."

"I thought you would, so here it is. This is a big night for me. I got a lot of industry friends here. Important people—unlike you. And the last thing I want is for any of them to get the idea that I'm some kinda uncivilized brute because I had to beat the livin' Christ outa some investigator who crashed my fuckin' party. It wouldn't look good. It's not how things are done in Hollywood. It'd be almost as bad for my business as it would be for your face. You with me?"

"I'm with ya," I say.

"Good. Okay, so in an attempt to find an amenable resolution—a compromise if you will—here's my proposition. I'm gonna go upstairs and get a blowjob from that fine young piece a ass right over there. You can stick around, get a fresh drink, make nice, whatever. But when that drink's gone, you're gone. 'Cuz if I come back down here after my dick-suck and I still see you standin' here smellin' up the place, I'm gonna throw caution to the wind and fuck you all up regardless. Capiche?"

It's true what they say about a vampire being unable to turn or use his powers on a victim in their own home unless invited in. I don't know why it works that way, or who makes the rules, but that's how it is. I came uninvited, but Vin had just changed all that—"stick around" is all it takes. Now all bets are off.

"Sorry," I say, looking past the twin monster reflections that stare back at me from the tinted glass of his Ray-Bans. "I don't speak wop."

Vin's ugly grin goes on a starvation diet, getting thinner and whiter and uglier, like an anorexic chick. For a second I think he's going to swing at me, but to his credit, he maintains control. It takes everything he has, but he does it.

"I almost hope you're here when I come back. I really do," he says backing away and straightening his tie. "It might be worth it to have you here. But that's your call."

With this, he turns and goes back to the sex-bot blonde, who immediately comes out of sleeper mode and begins to purr and cling according to the dictates of her programming. I watch Vin guide her up the spiral staircase and disappear above.

I light a smoke, ignoring indignant stares from the health-conscious Hollywood set. A too-skinny brunette with wannabe actress written all over her takes notice and drifts over.

"That looks really good," she tells me. "You have an extra?"

I shake one out, light it for her.

"Thanks," she blows smoke. "I'm supposed to've quit. These

things'll kill ya, y'know?"

"It's okay," I say. "I'm already dead."

She laughs. She thinks I'm joking. I let her keep thinking it.

"You're funny." There's nothing there for me so I just nod and smile.

"So what d'ya do for a living?"

"I salt slugs," I say, sizzling my own cigarette out in the last gulp of champagne at the bottom of my flute. "Excuse me."

I head upstairs. The hall is long and dark. Ornate Persian rugs hang from the walls. I try two oak doors, which open into empty bedrooms. Then I decide to see what's behind door number three.

What's behind it is a tastefully decorated room complete with a Juliet balcony, all-natural hardwood floors, an antique maple bureau, and a large four post canopy bed, where—true to his word—my new friend is playing bob-for-cock with the blonde. Both are so involved in what she's doing, they don't hear me come in.

I drift over to the bed where the dame, black cocktail dress in a flat-tire ring around her taut abs, kneels on the floor. I bend. I grab her by the elbow and pull. Her swollen lips come off Vin's small purple pecker with a slobbery-suctiony pop as I tug her to her feet and set her in motion.

"Let's go, doll. Me and Vinnie here need to talk."

"Hey," she says in protest, wiping at the drool that slimes her chin.

Behind the glasses, Vin's eyes snap open angry-like. "What

the fuck?"

Seeing me there, a look of cagey fear crosses his face, but it doesn't last. Rage and humiliation set in and he lunges off the bed at me, his dick moving up and down like a tiny diving board.

"You motherfucker—"

What he says next is hard to decipher because I've stopped his forward momentum at arm's length by grabbing him around the throat and clamping tight on his windpipe, but it sounds something along the lines of "Aack."

"Go on, honey. Get dressed and get out."

"Vin? Are you okay, baby?"

"Aaack," he says again, which I assure her means that he's just fine and he'll be along shortly.

Pulling her dress up and down as needed, she backs from the room, politely closing the door behind her. When she's gone, I yank Vin close so his face is scant inches from mine. I pull off his sunglasses and break them with my free hand. "Now you're gonna answer those questions we talked about. Capiche?"

He nods enthusiastically, even throws in a couple of "Aacks" to show me just how committed he is to the idea. I let him go. He sags like a sack of shit onto the bed. He sucks for air, one hand going to his throat while the other tugs his lipstick-stained shirttail down over his now-limp dick.

"Where'd you learn to do that?" he asks hoarsely. Oddly, he seems a little impressed with me.

"Kindergarten. It was a tough neighborhood."

"Well it was really something. No shit."

"Glad you liked it."

"I gotta tell ya, you're a lot stronger than you look, guy. Hey, you ever think about being in a movie? Guy like you, with your kinda—what's the word—demeanor and physicality, you could do well. I even got a movie in mind."

"No thanks," I say. Most movies are crap these days anyway. I haven't really liked one since black-and-white went out of style.

"No thanks? Whaddya mean? You don't wanna be in a movie? Everyone wants to be in a movie."

"Not me."

"Well lemme tell you about it at least. This movie I've got comin' up, it's about this guy, an ex-special forces operative, real badass who loses his wife and kid—"

That's all I hear of the plot because I've gone back to choking him. "You're not listening, Vinnie. I don't want to be in your two-bit movie. What I do want is to ask you some questions and get some answers in return. And that's all I want. Get me?"

He nods. He gets me.

"All right. I'm gonna let you go, but if anything comes out of your mouth that's anything besides an answer to one of my questions I'm gonna choke you unconscious, bring you around, and start all over. We clear?"

More nods. I let him go. His bagpipe lungs wheeze out an ugly Scottish dirge.

"Whaddya wanna know?" He winces, realizing he has already fucked up, but I let it go.

"Raya. Where is she?"

"I don't know."

Smells like the truth, but it's hard to be sure. The problem with guys like Vin Prince is they lie so damn much there's a constant stink about them.

"Have you heard from her since she left?"

"Yeah. Once."

"When?"

"Two—three weeks ago."

I wait for him to go on. He doesn't.

"What'd she want?"

"I don't remember."

I shake my head, disappointed-like, and make to start choking him again, but he flails backward onto the bed, hands held protectively to his throat.

"Okay, okay, I'll tell ya. I'll tell ya. She wanted—she wanted the number for my dealer."

"And?"

He shrugs. "I gave it to her."

"You gave a fourteen year-old kid the number for your meth dealer?"

"What am I, her daddy? I mean fuck, I was doing a whole lot worse than that by her age."

The mere mention of a fix reminds me that I haven't had one in a while. Alone in the quiet room with Vin, my hunger awakens like a colicky newborn. I find myself staring hard at the swollen, finger-reddened pulse in his neck. It has the same effect on me as that little old bell of Pavlov's.

"What are you lookin' at?"

If Vin hadn't invited me to stay downstairs, he'd have

nothing to worry about, but he did. He did, and now I feel the change pushing for release from whatever dark place it resides in. It rushes over me. The sheer intensity is shocking. I try to tell myself that Vin Prince might be a slime-bag—is a slime-bag—but that's not enough to buy him a death sentence. I have rules. Without my rules I'm just another mindless animal, but it's no use. I'm too weak to resist it. Even reminding myself what a bad idea it would be, that the blonde has seen me and knows I'm up here, isn't enough to stop it. I want to change. I want to sink my fangs deep into his throat and drink him dry like a spider does a fly.

Then I think of Reesa. I think of her lovely face and the way she made me feel and the investigation I'm supposed to be conducting on her behalf and somehow, amazingly, unbelievably, I manage to pull back at the very brink. The pain of abortion is hollow and immense. With a sort of growl, I tear my gaze from Vin's throat and back away toward the door, not trusting myself to be any closer.

"Y-You okay, pal?"

"I'm fine."

"You sure? You looked a little—I dunno—crazy there for a second. No offense," Vin laughs. Not "Ha-ha" but "Oh fuck".

"I said I'm fine," I say, as I wipe beads of perspiration from my brow. I have to focus.

"The girl. Did she call your dealer?"

"I don't know. Don't know, don't fucking care. Fuck her and her skeezebag sister."

I want to tell him he shouldn't talk about a lady like that, but I'm afraid if I open my mouth now what might come out instead is a lot of sharp teeth and murder. I buy some time by focusing on my trembling hands and forcing them to take pad and pen from my pocket.

"Your dealer—what's his name?"

I try to sound in control of myself, but it's a bluff, and a piss-poor one at that. I need to get out of here quick. The hunger has receded, but it isn't gone. I feel it crouched back and coiled to pounce like a tiger lying in wait. Vin seems to sense it. He tells me what I want to know. "Leroy. Leroy Watkins."

Pressing much too hard, I scratch it down. "Give me his number."

Vin gives it to me.

"You better not be jerking me around, Vin. You won't like it if I have to come back."

Time to go.

I leave Vin looking awfully pale for a guy with a year-round tan.

4

Back at the car I binge-fix until I feel in control of myself again. Well, as in control as I ever feel anyway. For a vampire there is always a disquieting sense that the wrong sequence of events at the wrong time could cause things to spiral out of control, like what almost happened back there with Vin. I imagine it's similar to what sharks experience when they scent blood in the water, or what a bull feels when the matador snaps his cape. A siren call to action that cannot be resisted. Consequences be damned.

Sleepy-eyed, I lull in the driver's seat. A Louis Armstrong trumpet solo fills the car. Of all the instruments, I love the trumpet best. It's what I played in the band in the time before. Not like Old Satchmo, but I played. I love the violent-kindness of the brass. Like a smack delivered for your own good. I love the way a well-played staccato burst can shoot you in the head one minute and raise you from the dead the next. I haven't touched a trumpet since 1943. Don't need to. That was the year I became one.

The solo ends. I shake the fog off and start the car. I take moon-scrubbed surface streets over to Hollywood to the club Reesa told me about; a place called the Tomb Room. I find it a block off Sunset, tucked in between a Mexican restaurant and a nail salon, right where Reesa said it would be. I park and walk back.

The music oozing like toxic waste from inside is almost enough to turn me around and head me right back home. I brace myself against the toxicity and move past a line of pasty-looking undead wannabes. Every one of them is dressed in black. Up and down the line both guys and girls wear heavy black eye makeup, black lipstick and black nail polish. The androgynous nature of the look makes it difficult to tell the sexes apart. Maybe that's the point, but it makes me wonder exactly when people got the idea that in order to look like a vampire you had to adopt a transvestite-in-mourning look. If these kids are looking for recruitment into the ranks, they're going about it the wrong way. Call me old-fashioned, but in my opinion the last thing the vampire world needs is a bunch of gender-confused losers who mistake being sullen and whiny for rebellious and interesting.

I skip to the head of the line, where a bouncer with sharpened teeth and a face full of tats and metal piercings stands by the door. To me it looks like a fishhook grenade blew up in his face. Topping the look off, two metal spikes sprout like devil horns from his bald head. He takes in my suit and fedora and looks at me like I'm the freak.

Maybe I am.

"You sure you're in the right place, guy?"

I nod in the affirmative and give him the eye. "Mick Angel. I'm on the list." He looks, finds my name right where it's not, and lifts the black velvet cordon to let me in. I enter through a black door into a black entryway illuminated by black lights.

There, a Morticia Addams look-alike checks my I.D. and demands fifteen bucks from me. I cough up, hardly able to believe I'm doing it considering what I'm about to subject my ears to. She affixes a black plastic wristband to my wrist and directs me through a thick black curtain into the main room. Imagine my surprise when it turns out to be painted all black.

The place is packed solid with kids. On the far side, on a black stage, back-dropped by a black banner depicting a gaping set of bloody fangs, a crew of music haters torture their instruments. The band looks as if they could have been plucked minutes ago right from the line outside. Judging by their musical ability, I wouldn't be too surprised to learn that was the case. According to the face of the drummer's bass drum, the band goes by the name Bite Me. Clever.

Ignoring looks and smirks and nudges from the peanut gallery, I make my way across a black floor over to a black bar. To get into the spirit of things I order Johnny Walker Black.

The bartender brings me my drink. It looks like he shares a butcher with the door guy. The main distinction I see is that instead of two metal spikes like horns, this guy has a ridge of spikes running down the center of his skull like a Mohawk. Cute.

I fat tip him for his trouble, then I pull the picture of Raya from my pocket and show it to him. "Recognize her?" I ask, needing to practically yell to be heard over the band.

He bends, looks, shakes his head, answers too fast. "Nope."

The lie hits me in the face like a slap from a dame. Before he can get away, I reach out and grab hold of the thick metal bullring that dangles under his nose.

It'd be nice if the gaze worked for eliciting information from people, but it doesn't. It's a handy tool, but only good for giving orders and altering memories. Information I have to finagle. Or force.

"Look again," I say, making my eyes dangerous; putting the promise of pain and the possibility of a very violent death in my eyes.

He looks.

"You've seen her in here?"

"Yeah. I've seen her."

"How long ago?"

"Three weeks maybe—"

"She come in a lot?"

"Used to, 'til we figured out she was using a fake I.D. Then we had to take it away and keep her out."

"Who does she hang out with? Anyone here tonight? Look."

I let the pull-tab go so he can browse the crowd. Finally he shakes his demon head and shrugs. "She used to come in with another kid, a little older than her. He comes in a lot, but I don't see him tonight."

Figuring he's talking about the eighteen year-old boyfriend, I take a stab. "This kid—his name Scotty?"

"Yeah, yeah, somethin' like that."

Now I give him the gaze. "I'm gonna be here for a while. You see him come in, you let me know."

"I'll let you know."

"Good boy," I tell him. "And keep the booze comin'. On you."

"On me," he says, ambling back into the shadows at the back of the bar.

I sit. I drink. I smoke. No one at this fleabag seems to give enough of a shit about a bad habit as mainstream as smoking to come hassle me. Maybe the joint isn't so bad after all.

Time passes. A skinny, strung-out dame in all-black everything comes to the bar for a drink. She takes in my suit and fedora and tells me I remind her of her dad.

"Yeah? That turn you on?" I ask.

She shrugs. "Kinda."

"Well that's funny because you remind me of my dead ex-wife." It's not a lie, she does. A little. Most places an admission like that would be a conversation stopper. Not here.

"Really? Cool. How'd she die?"

"I killed her. I didn't want to, but she made me." That does the trick. Next time I look, Skinny and her drink are gone.

Bite Me goes off, but their sound is all-too-soon replaced by an even worse racket created by a band calling themselves the Sinister Ministers, who take to the stage in white-collared priest get-ups.

I go to the black-walled bathroom and pick a black stall and fix. I guess I'm in there too long because someone outside pounds on the door and asks if I'm giving birth in there. I put my kit away and fake flush. I exit to find a kid with long unkempt black hair, black nails, and black lipstick waiting outside.

"'Bout time," he says.

I look him up and down. Call me old fashioned, but I liked it when men went around looking like men. This kid looks like a skirt. An ugly one.

"You sure you're in the right bathroom?" I ask him.

"You sure you're in the right decade?" he fires back.

Touché. I nod, shrug, go to the sink, wash up. When I get back to my freshly-refilled drink at the bar, the bartender comes over and gently taps me on the shoulder. He jabs one sharp-taloned finger at a black-haired Cousin It lookalike standing arms-crossed next to a back exit.

"That's him. That's the kid the girl you showed me was always with."

I thank him, and cut a circus-freak swath over to the kid. I try to be sly about it but it's no good, I stand out like a tick at a flea convention and he sees me coming. Taking me for a cop, he turns and ducks out the door before I can collar him.

I hit the piss-stinking alley only a handful of steps behind him.

"Scotty!"

He looks back without slowing, his long jet-black hair flaps like a cape as he runs full-tilt-boogie toward the street. Fueled by meth and who knows what all else, he's fast, but he's still no match for a real vampire. I catch up in a matter of steps, grab hold of that mile of hair, and yank. Hard. His head stops, but the rest of him doesn't. His feet fly out in front of him and he back-flops onto the cracked black asphalt with a lung-collapsing *oof*. Looks painful.

Before anyone can come out and see us I drag him, helpless and incapacitated, into the shadows behind the rusty dumpster at the back of the Mexican restaurant.

I stand over the kid as he sucks in shallow gasps of air. His black New York Dolls band t-shirt rides up, exposing his midriff. He is impossibly skinny; a skeleton in black jeans. His boyish face is about a hundred years younger than the world-wise eyes that stare out of it, but a few more years on the street, it'll catch up. Faces always do.

"I'm not holdin'. Fuckin' search me if you want," he says when his wind is back and he can form words again.

"I'm not a cop."

"Then what the fuck do you want with me, man?"

I take the picture of Raya out and stick it in his drug-sweaty face. "I'm lookin' for this girl. I know you know her. Where can I find her?"

"I dunno, man. I haven't seen her."

I don't smell a lie, but his fear could be covering it up. To cover my bases, I take the .38 out and press it up under his weak chin. I give him the scary eye; the same one I gave the bartender.

"Like I said, I'm not a cop, which means I don't have to follow any rules here. So shoot me straight if you know what's good for you."

"I am, dude. I swear. I haven't seen Raya in weeks."

"What happened to her?"

"I dunno. She was here, then she was gone. Maybe that bitch

did somethin' to her."

"This town has more bitches than traffic lights. Which bitch are you referring to?"

"The bitch she was staying with."

"Raya was living with someone?"

He nods.

"Who?"

"I only know her by her stripper name."

I look at him expectantly.

"Dallas. She went by Dallas."

"What club did she work?"

"I dunno. I only met her once, but I didn't trust her."

"Why not?"

He shrugs and says, "You live on the street you either get a sense about people or else ya don't live on the street long. There was something off about her. She promised Raya all kindsa shit she was gonna do for her. Get her off the streets. Help her get her GED. It sounded like bullshit to me. Too good to be true, ya know?"

I nod. I know all right.

"Anyway, the bitch offered Raya a place to stay and Raya took it. Even started calling Dallas her big sister. I guess she was looking for one after what her real sister did to her."

"What'd she do?"

"Raya and her sister were livin' with some producer guy. Can't remember his name—"

"Vin Prince."

"Yeah, him. They were livin' with that asshole and one day

while her sister was out he got high on meth and raped Raya. Sister came home in the middle of it, saw them together and took his side. Kicked Raya out for screwing her boyfriend. How's that for fucked?"

It was fucked all right; if it was true. My blood does the old slow boil just thinking about how hard I fought to keep from killing Prince when, as it turns out, I might've been doing the world a favor if I had.

"Did you go to the police when Raya went missing?"

"No. Why would I?"

"Your friend disappeared."

Despite the gun, the kid laughs and looks at me like I'm half retarded. "C'mon, dude. The fuckin' pigs don't give a shit about street kids unless they can bust one of us for drugs. One of us turns up dead, the most they do is contact next of kin. Fuck the police."

"Right," I say. I feel a little bit bad for the kid. He doesn't seem like a bad sort, just un-fucking-lucky. I take the picture back and put the gun away and pull some of the money Reesa gave me out. I peel off a twenty and stretch it out to him. "Here. For your trouble."

His eyes go wide and greedy seeing it. He starts to take it, but stops himself like a stray offered food from a hand that has hit it one too many times. His eyes grow wary, wondering if maybe I want a little something extra for the cash.

"Go on, take it. It's yours, free and clear."

Hardly able to believe it, he takes the bill in both hands. "Aw fuck man, thanks. I can really use this. Thanks. Thanks, dude."

I nod and turn to go.

"Hey," the kid says, stopping me at one sharp corner of the dumpster. "You see that Vin guy, tell 'im he's a fucking asshole for me, huh?"

"Sure, kid," I say.

Then I'm gone.

Normally a vampire's sleep is like death; total immersion in the black waters of oblivion where there is no light, no awareness, no dreams. It's why vampires are so vulnerable in their sleep state. Because it's more than sleep. Occasionally, however, dreams get through. Maybe it's meeting the girl that did it. Maybe it's the unexpected nostalgia brought on by the stops I made. Maybe it's talking about her with the skinny girl in the club that shoveled up a long-buried memory best forgotten. Whatever the case—tonight I dream. I dream of the past. Of 1943. And a twist name of Coraline.

1943

Things with Coraline began with a bullet.

Like thousands of other small-town beauty queens who have been told all of their small-town lives that they're pretty enough be in pictures, she had come to Hollywood seeking fame and fortune.

As a child, her favorite book had been *The Wonderful Wizard of Oz*. I remember her telling me how she had read it over and over until the pages wilted and fell out like flower petals from a dead bouquet. The only part of the book she didn't like was the end, where Dorothy returns home. Coraline told me she had ripped that chapter out the first time through. She thought Dorothy was a dumb bitch for giving up Oz for Kansas. A dumb bitch. That was how she put it.

Maybe the book captivated her for the simple reason that she, like Dorothy, was a small-town Kansas girl. Maybe it was something more sinister than that. Like the stumbling drunk of a dad who she never talked to and refused to say much about.

Whatever the case, Coraline knew she wanted the hell out of Kansas from an early age. She wanted something more from life. Something bigger. It was this that led her to Hollywood in March of '43. And to me.

She had only been in town maybe a month or two by then. I met her on a break between sets at a Boyle Heights dive bar where the boys and me had been hired to fill an off week. I saw her across the smoke-filled room seated at a four-top near the bar. She was sitting by her plain Jane friend, smoking a cigarette in a way that made you just know she thought she was doing something bad and was enjoying it all the more because of it. It made me smile and our eyes met and she smiled back like she was in on the joke.

I've always been a cynic. I'd never believed in love at first sight until that moment. 'Til then I'd thought it was just some sappy concept thought up by some no-talent screenwriter somewhere. Maybe this was the real thing and maybe it wasn't, but goddamn it was close. My first sight of Coraline took hold of me like my first veinful of dope. Her hair, pulled up in a trendy forward-curled pompadour, was the blue-black of a crow's wing at midnight. It struck an uneasy alliance with her powder-pale skin. Dark eyebrows set off a pair of jewel-blue eyes. A pert, slightly upturned nose was balanced on a teeter-totter of kissable red lips. The moment I saw her I was hooked. I knew if given the chance I would keep going back to that well no matter the cost. Even if it poisoned me.

I went over and introduced myself. She told me her name was Coraline. She told me she'd heard about me and the boys and how she had snuck out past curfew from the boarding house where she lived just to come see us. She told me she thought we were swell, just swell. Then the girls' dates came back from the bar armed with drinks and scowls and things got a little awkward. They got even more awkward when I asked Coraline to accompany me to a private party I knew of after the show.

"Hey, what are you tryin' to pull, Dad? Can't you see she's spoken for?" Coraline's date, a wisp of a kid, demanded. He had a bang of muddy blond hair and a weak jaw and I didn't blame him a bit for trying to hold on to her. I knew as soon as I saw her that Coraline was the kind of girl bucks locked horns over.

My eyes never left Coraline's. "No one's talkin' to you, Junior, so why don't you just do yourself a favor and sit there quietly while the girl makes up her own mind."

He was too young and dumb to know it, but I was doing him a favor. No way a lightweight like him could handle a gal like that. If I hadn't stepped in she'd have K-Oed him before the end of round two. A girl like her was best left to a seasoned masochist like myself.

"You hard a hearin', Dad? I said she's spoken for." The kid clapped a skinny mitt down on my shoulder.

Before I turned away, I saw the look of anticipation and excitement that flooded Coraline's eyes. It was the look of a girl having a fantasy realized. She had been waiting all her life to have something like this to write down in her diary.

No doubt the kid probably had some tough-guy line he'd

seen in a movie ready to deliver, but he never got to it on account of my fist connecting with his nose. There was an ugly crunch and he jitterbugged backward a few steps and crashed down hard atop an adjoining table, overturning it with a crash.

I reared around on his big moose of a buddy, who looked ready to try his luck, but I guess the sight of Morris and the other boys hurrying over to get my back changed his mind. Black faces have a way of doing that to white boys. Even big dumb ones. Instead of taking a swing, the moose bent and helped his hurt friend up. Maybe he wasn't as dumb as he looked.

By then the bar's bouncers were there and began hustling the younger guys toward the exit. Under normal circumstances I'd probably have been tossed out on my ear too—I'd been the one to throw the first punch after all—but then I was with the band and we still had a set to play.

Amid all the hubbub, I turned back to Coraline. I wanted to make sure the sudden violence hadn't put the brakes on things. It hadn't. I found her looking at me, eyes glowing brighter than a welder's torch, a crooked halo smile perched on her lips. I'd never been looked at by a woman that way before. I'd been looked at all kinds of ways—lots of them bad—but not like that. Coraline was staring at me like she saw in me the potential for some darker life she'd always secretly desired, but had been too timid to seek. Like I was the answer to some pagan prayer. Like I was her cigarette all come to life.

I stared right back. I guess maybe I saw all the same things in her. I guess maybe that's why I'd come over in the first place. And I guess maybe that's why I never saw the kid pull the gun from the waistband of his loose-fitting chinos and shoot me in the back.

The bullet, a .22, pierced my right lung and lodged in a rib. The sawbones who patched me up told me if it had been just a hair to the left it would've paralyzed me. A touch lower and it would've killed me. I guess it was supposed to make me feel lucky. It didn't.

I spent an angry month in the hospital. Coraline came to visit me every day. By the end of my stay there, I was completely in love. I had thought I had been in love before her, but I was wrong. Dead wrong. The passion I had felt for other dames was a ghost emotion compared to how I felt about Coraline; insubstantial, barely there. This was something else. Something fearsome in its depth and complexity. I was weak for her in a way I'd never been with any other woman, in a way I didn't even know I could be. If she had asked, I would have killed, died, even sold my soul for her.

In the end I guess I did all three.

Once I was released, Coraline and I decided it might be fun to play house together. It was. We rented a cheap little bungalow in Venice just a few blocks off the beach. Caught up in the excitement of it all, we even went and hunted up a Justice of the Peace and made it official. It was my idea. Call me old-fashioned, but I couldn't stand the idea of people looking down their noses at my girl. I wanted to make an honest woman of her. If only it had been that easy.

For a while, things were good—real good, if you want to know the truth. I played music with the boys, and Coraline went on auditions during the day and came to watch our shows at night. She liked the late-night lifestyle and the fast crowd I ran with. She liked the parties and the drinking. She liked it all.

Problem was, my love for Coraline wasn't the only thing I took with me when I left the hospital. The bullet had hurt like hell, hurt like nothing I'd ever experienced before, and after a month of treatment, the morphine the docs gave me for the pain had begun to seem more a necessity than a luxury. Once I hit the street, I starting buying heroin because it was cheaper and easier to get, but it all came to the same thing in the end. I was an addict.

I tried to hide it from her, and I had done a pretty swell job of it until she walked in on me in the bathroom one night after we had gotten back from a show at Club Alabam, a needle still dangling from my arm. Your typical dame would have yelled, thrown things, demanded I go and seek treatment, but Coraline was anything but typical. Looking back on it, it seems she had been waiting her whole life for the right twister to come along and sweep her off to Oz. Thanks to me, she found it in heroin.

"I want to try it," she said, as I attempted to hide my kit along with my humiliation.

"No, that's a bad idea, baby."

"Why? It's okay for you, but not for me?"

"It's not okay for anyone, but I can stop. I'll quit. I swear it."

"I didn't ask you to quit, Mick. I just asked you to share."

"I'm not doing that."

"Fine. Then I'll just go out and find someone who will. Is

that what you want? Me to go out and look for it on my own? Is it?"

Coraline could be stubborn sometimes. Real stubborn, if you want to know the truth. I knew her well enough by then to know that when she sounded like that there was no point in arguing. She wasn't bluffing. She would do what she said. So I gave in. I wish to God I hadn't, but I did. She clapped her hands together like a little girl who has been told she's getting a pony on her birthday.

I had to shoot her up that first time because of her aversion to needles. I remember the way she looked at me, a beatific, sleepy-eyed expression on her face. I remember her exact whispered words after I pressed the plunger home. "We're not in Kansas anymore, Toto."

Got to give it to her, she was right. This was Oz. Except in this version the bricks were black and the road led straight to hell. Funny. I had thought I was protecting her by not letting her try it, but I soon found out it was me I was protecting all along. Although I didn't know it yet, heroin had taken my place in her affections and things would never be the same.

Over the course of the next few months we sunk into addiction together like panicky swimmers who drag each other beneath the waves. Larger and larger quantities of our time went to scraping together the cash to buy. With two sizeable addictions to feed, it was no easy task. Pretty soon I found I wasn't in a band anymore. I pawned my trumpet. Why not? It was no good to me just sitting around. When that money was gone I brushed up on my lock-picking skills and turned to breaking and entering. But in the end it was Coraline who became the real breadwinner by selling the one thing she had to sell—her body. It killed me to let her do it, but the dope it provided helped me forget.

With her looks and that body, it wasn't long before Coraline had built a fairly sizeable number of steady clients, many of them key players in the film industry willing to pay good money for a quickie with a discreet gal. Most times I went along with her on her "dates," to make sure no one got out of line. One particular night, however, I shot too much and got too high and Coraline drove out to a certain producer's Hollywood Hills house alone. She came back three hours later with her lovely china doll face all beat to hell. Always a gentleman in the past, the bastard had gotten drunk and mean this time around.

One eye swollen shut, the left side of her face a violent tale in Braille, I listened with growing rage as Coraline filled me in around a fat lip. I'd grown up watching my mom take regular beatings from my dad until it killed her. I didn't believe in laying hands on a woman, and I sure as hell wasn't about to let some rich Hollywood asshole get away with doing it to mine. I went and grabbed the snub-nosed .38 I kept under the mattress for protection.

"Let's go see him."

She looked at me, curious. "What are you gonna do to him?"

"I'm gonna beat him until his face looks like yours and then I'm gonna beat him some more."

"I have a better idea. He's rich. You know how you hurt a

guy like that, baby? You take his money. He got screwed by the banks back in '29 and now he keeps all his cash in a wall safe in his house. I saw it. He paid me out of it once. I'd never seen so much money in my whole life. We do this, our money troubles will be over."

I should have said no. If I had everything would have been different, but I didn't. I was mad—mad as hell, if you want to know the truth—and she was preaching to the choir.

"Let's compromise. We'll do both."

We piled into the black Packard we were driving then and drove to the Hills for a little social call. The house—a tall two-story number with ivy-covered white-stone walls, a terracotta roof, and an arched entryway— looked like a thousand others stabbed down along the twisting roads that snaked through the Hollywood Hills.

We knocked. No one came to the door, so Coraline and I let ourselves in. We found him passed out on the living room couch, knuckles still covered with Coraline's dried blood. He was a big fella, but the muscle of his youth had turned to a jelly-like fat from years of overindulgence and good eating. He woke up to the barrel of my .38 doing a Woody Woodpecker routine on his forehead. His expression went from surly to worried in the time it took him to recognize Coraline through her swollen features and take note of the gun.

"I'm back, Roy, and I've brought a friend," Coraline said over my shoulder. "What's wrong? Aren'tcha happy to see me, lover?"

He didn't look happy. Scared. Confused certainly. Not happy.

"Whaz'is?" he asked, his words still slurred by drink. "Whaz goin' on?" He looked back and forth between us. I let Coraline do the explaining. She was always the better explainer.

"Look at my face, Roy. Look what you did to me. I came over to show you a nice time and look what you went and did."

"I shouldn't've done thzat."

"No. You shouldn't have. So now you're going to have to pay for it. That's what grownups do after all, isn't it? Pay for their mistakes."

"How much d'you wan'?"

"Well, I'm not going to be able to work for a while looking like I do, so you're going to have to pay me disability. It could get expensive."

"How much?"

"Make you a deal. Let's go into your safe. You start paying and I'll tell you when my face stops hurting."

"I'm not opening my g'damn safe for nobody."

"I'm sorry to hear that," Coraline said, with a look at me. "I suppose you'd better hurt him, Mick."

I hurt him. I was happy to do it. I pistol-whipped the fat drunk bastard until his face matched Coraline's and then I pistol-whipped him some more. He was sobbing like a huge overgrown baby by the time Coraline grabbed my wrist and made me stop. A slick mixture of blood, snot and saliva dripped from Roy's nose and mouth, staining his expensive linen shirt.

"I'm sorry. I'm sorry. I'm sorry. I'm sorry."

"It's all right, Roy. I forgive you. It's over. All you have to do is be a good boy and give us the combination to the safe and I won't let him hurt you any more. I promise," Coraline cooed.

Battered as he was, Roy still hesitated. I raised the gun again, and the numbers came spilling out like a jackpot in a Vegas slot.

We herded him at gunpoint into the mahogany world of the office. The safe was in the wall, behind a portrait of Roy's homely mother. Pulling it from the wall, he made as if to go and open the safe, but I pushed him aside. I didn't want to take the chance he might have a gun of his own hidden within. I handed the .38 to Coraline, told her to cover him, and spun the small black dial. The safe popped open first time round, revealing a stash of cash the likes of which I'd never seen outside of the movies, and a small black pistol.

Shaking a disappointed finger at Roy, I turned back to the safe and began to toss the cash—what looked at a glance to be about forty grand or so— into the bag we'd thought to bring. When it was empty I closed it and zipped the bag and smiled at Coraline.

She didn't notice. She was too busy staring down the barrel of the .38 at Roy. The way her one eye was swollen shut gave the impression she was taking careful aim.

"We've got the money, but my face still hurts, Roy," she said regretfully.

"Coraline—" I interrupted.

"Yes, darling?"

"This wasn't the plan," I said.

"Stay out of it, Mick. It's not your face he beat up. It's not you it happened to."

I had to admit that it wasn't. Still, this wasn't the plan.

"Put the gun down, baby."

"No."

"Why not?"

She smiled. "I don't want to. And besides, he knows my name. He can finger us. We walk out of here he'll have the police on us in an hour."

"No I won't. I won't. You can have the money. I don't care about it," Roy sounded a lot more sober as he pleaded for his life.

"He says that now, but we leave, he'll start to care, Mick. It's a lot of money. He'll care and he'll call the cops. You know he will."

I knew it, despite the vehement way Roy was shaking his chins at me. Still, killing people—even ones who maybe could do with killing—wasn't my style. Not back then anyway. We had his money. We'd given him a beating. It was enough.

"We'll tie him up," I said. "We'll go to Mexico. By the time he works himself free we'll be across the border."

"I don't want to live in Mexico," Coraline said.

"Canada then."

Coraline shook her head. "Not there either. I like it right here." She looked highly satisfied about things as she cocked the gun.

Roy went all pie-eyed. I didn't know eyes could get that wide.

"You promised you wouldn't hurt me if I went along," he said. "You promised."

Coraline shook her head and smiled like a teacher speaking to a confused student. "No, Roy. What I promised was that I wouldn't let Mick do it," she said sweetly.

The crack of the gun left a ringing like alarm bells in my ears.

6

Next night I awaken with a severe hemoglobin hangover. Old blood has a way of doing that to you. Maybe the binging I did wasn't such a great idea. In fact I'm sure of it.

I go to the mini-fridge. I pry the door open. I take stock. It doesn't take long. Only two measly vials left. Damn. Two vials would be a modest nightly allotment, but now I'm going to have to stretch them. I curse my weakness. Then I decide to forgive myself and fix. I'm not one to hold a grudge, especially against someone I like as much as me.

I gather my tools together and sort myself out. Better. I might not be feeling like a million bucks, but at least I'm drawing interest again. I go get dressed. On the way past, I punch the play messages button on my machine. There is a message waiting for me from a Detective Coombs. He wants to talk to me. Just a few routine questions about a case he's working on. Give him a call back at my convenience. Yada, yada, yada.

I'm not in the habit of talking to cops. They make me

uneasy. Always have. If he wants me, he'll just have to run me down. I erase the message and turn my attention to picking out an ensemble.

A sharp rap sounds at the door as I re-knot my tie for the fourth and final time. I stash my kit and go answer it. A familiar-looking rumpled Schmo in an off-the-rack suit stands there. He's about my height, but fatter, balder, and has the look and smell of bacon about him.

"Detective Coombs."

"That's right. Good guess. You Michael Angel?"

I nod. I'm not in the habit of talking to cops.

"Can I come in?"

I nod again. Then I step aside to let him enter and shut the door and point him to a chair. He sits, and rubs his arms together for warmth.

"Kinda cold in here, isn't it?"

"I like it," I say, sinking like depression into my own chair across the desk from him. I don't bother to explain that as a vampire I keep it that way to slow my decay. I figure that information is need-to-know only and he don't need to know.

Coombs is irritated, but gives me a suit-yourself shrug. He stares across the desk at me a minute, then cocks his head, and gives me a puzzled look. "Have we met somewhere?"

"Oh I think I'd remember that," I say.

Coombs has been a homicide detective for more years than he has chins and the truth is we've met on two previous occasions. This makes three. Another thing he don't need to know.

He nods. "Yeah," he says. "Yeah. Anyway, uh, I called earlier but you didn't get back to me. Hope you don't mind my just dropping by like this."

I do, but I don't bother to mention it.

"Oh, yeah, well I didn't get your message until now. I just got in."

"That so? You sure about that?"

"Yeah, sure I'm sure."

"Well, the reason I ask is I've been parked out front for a while now. You know, filling out paperwork and such, an' I didn't see you come in. I only came up because I figured I ought at least knock before I left."

"Yeah well, there's a back way. I use it to avoid bill collectors. And cops." He looks at my smile like it's a new undiscovered species of expression. "That was a joke."

"Oh, I gotcha. Funny."

I light a cigarette, offer him the pack, but he shakes me off. "So what is it I can do for you, Detective?"

"Oh, well, see, like I said, I'm just running down some details on a case I'm working on."

"Interesting case?"

"Oh I think so. 'Course, then I think all murder investigations are pretty interesting."

"Murder huh?"

"The big M."

"Anyone I know?"

"Funny, I was just gonna ask you that question. Dead guy goes—went I should say—by the name Michael Ensinger. Ring a bell?"

I scrunch my brow all up in a way I hope appears I'm giving this some real thought, then shake my head and say: "Nope. Should it?"

"Well, guy was in the *Times* a while back. He got arrested for stalking and raping a girl by the name of Elizabeth Lowery. Hurt her pretty bad too."

"If he got arrested, what was he doing out?"

"He got off. Girl wouldn't testify. Too scared."

I shrug. "Maybe she did it. You think a that?"

"We did, but I don't think decapitation would be her style."

"I really wouldn't know."

"So I guess that means you don't know Elizabeth Lowery either, huh?"

"Now look who's the good guesser."

The detective's face settles into a comfortable frown that looks very natural on him. "Where were you last Monday night?"

"Here."

"All night?"

I go through the big contemplative act again and nod. "Yeah, except for running a few errands."

"These errands, did they happen to take you by the fourteen-hundred block of Ivar?"

"No," I say too quickly.

Coombs notices, but pretends not to. "Well, the reason I ask is because I talked to a guy who says a red Mercedes matching the description of yours was seen parked just up the street from the crime scene."

There's nothing there for me so I just grunt.

"You do own a red mint-condition '57 Mercedes-Benz 300 SL Roadster, don't you?"

I feel my head nod a response.

"Yeah, see, we got lucky, 'cause this guy who saw it happens to be a real car buff. He lives in the area and he pulled over to really check it out. Even got a look at the plate." Coombs fishes some reading glasses out of one rumpled suit pocket and a notepad out of another. He puts the glasses on and flips the pad open and reads my plate number out to me. "That yours?"

The one drawback to having a one-of-a-kind set of wheels is people tend to notice.

"Yeah. It's mine," I say, with that sinking feeling that only comes when being interrogated by cops and women.

"Seems a funny coincidence, but I guess if you say you weren't there, then you weren't there."

Coombs sits back, scratches his Friar Tuck dome, and waits to see if I'll hang myself with the length of rope he's run out for me.

I snap my fingers like I've just had a thought. "Oh wait, did you say Monday night?"

"Yeah, Monday."

"Tuesday is when I ran the errands. But Monday, Monday I was near Ivar."

"Mind if I ask what you were doing there?"

"Just visiting a friend."

"Can I get the name of your friend? You know, for my records." He finds a pen and gets ready to write.

"I'd rather not say."

Coombs doesn't give me much, just raises his eyebrows a little. It's a neat trick. The awkward silence sits like a guilty plea between us, making me feel like I should explain, so I do. "See, my friend, she's a married woman. Her husband travels. She gets lonely. You know how it is."

"Oh I know," he nods. "Tell ya what. You give me her name and I'll be real discreet when I go talk with her. You have my word on that."

Okay, damage-control time. I'm reluctant to use the hypnotic gaze, not knowing how many people know what at this point, but the damn guy has me painted into a corner. Moving fast, I bolt out of my seat and smack the reading glasses off the detective's surprised face. There's a lot at stake. Can't take any chances on them screwing with the works. Floored by this development, Coombs sputters and spews and tries to jump out of the chair, but I pin him in place, stare deeply into his shit-brown eyes and say, "You're fine. Calm down."

"I'm fine," he says, growing calm.

"Nothing out of the ordinary has happened here."

"Nothing… "

"The woman's name is Marla Dupree."

"Marla Dupree," he mumbles.

"Write that down in your pad." He writes it. "You already went and talked with her."

"I talked with her."

"That's right, and Marla, she backed my story up. It all checked out."

"It checked out."

"Right. So, I'm no longer a suspect in this investigation. If it ever comes up you'll find a way to explain it all. But aside from that, you won't even think about me again after you leave here. We've never met. I don't even exist."

"Never met. Don't exist."

"That's right. Very good, Detective," I say, bending and retrieving his glasses from the floor. I set them back on his face and return to my chair and my cigarette. "Now I think we're done here, so why don'tcha scram."

Coombs stands abruptly, his meaty hamstrings screeching the chair back on the wood floor. "Scram," he says.

I watch from behind a veil of cigarette smoke as the Detective zombie-walks to the door and opens it. In the doorway, he stops and looks back at me, a bewildered smile spread on his face.

I smile, wave. "Nice talking with you, Detective."

"Uh yeah. Y-you too."

"Keep up the good work," I tell him as he steps out of my office, pulling the door shut behind him.

When he's gone, I sit and smoke and fret. Goddamn Michael Ensinger is turning out to be more trouble dead than alive.

I could just kill the guy.

7

"Can you tell me if Dallas is working tonight?"

"Who?"

"Dallas. I think that was her name. She danced for me the other night and I wanted to come in and see her again."

"No girls here by that name, pal, but we got lotsa others—"

"That's all right. Thanks anyway."

I hang up. I cross the number out in the book and move on to the next one. I've spent the last thirty minutes calling every strip club I can find a listing for. Working the phone is tedious, but sometimes it pays off. I'm an hour in and halfway through my third L.A. directory when it finally does. Dallas works at a joint called the Blue Veil in Hollywood. The woman's voice on the other end tells me Dallas will definitely be in later. I thank her and hang up.

I have some questions for Reesa so I head to the Tropicana where I am directed backstage to her dressing room. The star on the red painted door bears her name. I knock.

"Yes?"

"It's me. Mick."

"C'min."

The room is only half as big again as a good-sized walk-in closet, but it is crammed full with amenities that include a costume wardrobe, an old-timey dressing blind, a television, an antique bureau, a mini-fridge and a futon. I find her seated at the bureau, painting her face in the lighted mirror there. She wears the red silk kimono I like so much. From the way it folds open invitingly just below the neck I can tell she isn't wearing much underneath.

"Well this is a nice surprise," she says, standing and taking my hands in hers and painting my stubbly cheek with red brushstroke lips. "Oh, look what I've done," she says, rubbing out the lip-mark memento I would just as soon have kept. She takes my hat and directs me to the futon. "Sit. Make yourself comfortable."

Like a good soldier, I do as I'm told.

"Can I pour you a drink?"

"What have you got?" I ask.

With a sly smile, Reesa delves into a bureau drawer and comes out with an unopened bottle of Macallen Eighteen. "I asked the bartender what you drank after you left the other night. Hope you don't mind."

I don't and tell her so. She locates a couple of glasses, pours us each a healthy belt and hands me mine.

"To new friends," she says, glass held out.

"New friends," I agree.

We clink glasses. We drink. She pulls the bureau chair closer and sits so that our knees touch. Times like this I wish I had more feeling in my limbs.

I start to get a cigarette out, but stop. "You mind if I smoke?"

"Not so long as you share."

I stab two smokes between my lips, set them on fire, hand her one. She takes hold of it delicately, branding the tip with her lips like she did my cheek. "So, are you here on business or pleasure?"

"Business."

"That's too bad." She smiles. "Okay, what can I do for you?"

"Well, for starters, you can tell me why you lied to me."

The only tell that the remark has hit home is the slight catch of smoke in her throat. "What do you mean?"

"You told me Raya just ran away from Vin's. But that's not how it happened, is it?"

Long pause. "No," she says softly, eyes in her lap.

"How do you expect me to help you find your sister if you won't level with me?"

"I'm sorry," she says. "I shouldn't have lied."

"Why did you?"

I wait. The smoke from our cigarettes mingles like spirits in the air.

"Because. Because I was ashamed," she says, surprising me by meeting my eyes now. "I caught them together and even though I knew deep down what kind of man he was I took his side over hers. I was weak and scared of losing what I had with him so I blamed Raya." She shakes her head, blows smoke, shrugs. "The fact that you gave your own sister the boot after your boyfriend raped her isn't such an easy thing to tell a stranger in the first five minutes you've known him."

A tear makes a break for her jaw-line, but Reesa catches it and bats it angrily away. I can't tell if she's mad at herself or the tear or me. Maybe all three. "Now look what you've gone and done." She does her best to catch the other conspirators on the brink but there are too many for her and she gives up.

"I'm sorry. I just had to know."

"Well, now you do."

"I'm sorry," I say again, taking my own stab at wiping away the tears. I don't have any more luck than she did.

"You probably think I'm a horrible person to do something like that, don't you?"

"No," I say, meaning it. "You were a drug addict. Drug addicts do all kinds of things when they're hooked that they aren't proud of later. It goes with the territory."

There is a glimmer of recognition in her eyes. "You sound like you know."

"I know." When the kiss comes it takes me by surprise. So much so that I pull away. A fact that surprises me even more than the kiss.

"What's wrong? Don't you like me, Mick?"

"Sure I like you," I say. She has no idea.

"Well then?"

The statement sits like an unread contract between us. As tempted as I am to grab a pen and sign my name, I stand up instead. I've got rules about this sort of thing. A junkie like me can't go breaking his rules. Bad things happen once that starts.

"I can't."

"Why not?" She pouts all cute and girlish.

"I've got rules."

"What kind of rules?"

"About getting too involved."

"Does that go for clients or for everyone?"

"Take your pick," I say, looking around for where she put my hat. Why is it you can never find your goddamn hat when you're in a hurry?

Reesa stands now and kittens up to me. Her fingers walk my tie. "Well, you know what I always say—"

"What's that?" I ask, knowing I shouldn't; knowing I'm just opening the door for her to wedge one of those perfect little size six feet in it.

"Rules are like hymens—made to be broken." She grins, too cute for her own good. Too goddamn cute by half. My turn to smile.

"You always say that, huh?"

She shakes her head, making her red curls jingle and bounce. "Not really. First time." She looks me deep in the eyes, and blows smoke as she stubs her butt out in her glass. "Well, I guess if you feel that strongly about it then a kiss goodbye is out of the question."

I nod. "Completely."

She raises her face to kiss me anyway, her lips opening like flower petals in bloom.

"I'll mess your hair and makeup all up," I warn, our mouths almost touching now.

"It wouldn't be much worth doing if you didn't."

I grab hold of those curls and we kiss like an electric shock. Her mouth tastes of Scotch and smoke, which could be unpleasant but isn't. I haven't let myself get this close to a woman in ages because of my penchant for picking the wrong ones. Call it a knack. I am overwhelmed by fear and desire. It's been a long time since I've felt either. Since I've felt much of anything. The numbness that comes with being undead isn't just physical, it's emotional too. Anger is the one exception. There always seems to be plenty of that on hand. Maybe it's what makes us vampires capable of the things we're made to do. I don't know. What I do know is that right now with her I feel more alive than I have in longer than I care to consider.

"There, now that wasn't so bad, was it?" she asks when we part.

I don't trust myself to speak, so I just shake my head. I want more. Lots more, if you want to know the truth.

"Well, I'd ask you to stay, but I have a show to do in a half hour."

"And I have a girl to find." I locate my hat in plain sight on a low shelf and mash it on.

"How about if we get together later when we can take our time with things? I'm off tomorrow night."

I open my mouth to say forget it, but what comes out sounds a whole lot more like "Sure".

She grins playfully. "Your place or mine?"

"Better make it yours. I don't have a bed."

"You don't? Then where do you sleep?"

"In a freezer," I deadpan. She laughs. She thinks I'm joking. I let her keep thinking it. "Where's your place at?"

Reesa moves toward the dressing blind at the back of the room, unknotting the red silk belt that holds the matching kimono in check as she goes. She stops beside it, turns back to me. Red silk puddles like blood at her feet. I try to keep my eyes polite, but sometimes they get fresh all on their own. This is one of those times.

Clad only in a smile brimming with mischief, she shrugs. "You're a detective. Find me."

I need a pay phone. I aim the Benz for Canter's Deli. As I roll south down a car-barnacled Hollywood surface street an unchanging pair of headlights in the Benz's rearview makes me think I'm being tailed again. I take a couple of turns out of my way just to be sure. Whoever is following me doesn't know what the hell they're doing. The tail is too obvious and amateurish even for cops. So then who? The possibilities are practically endless. I haven't exactly been racking up acquaintances who would fall into the 'new friend' category just lately.

I take a right, then a quick left into a narrow alleyway that curls behind a set of overpriced condos. I pull in behind a brown dumpster and cut the lights. I don't have to wait long before my tail—a familiar-looking '77 Ford pick-up as it turns out—pulls in after me.

When I see he's committed, I throw the Roadster into reverse and punch it, hoping I can get close enough to at least get a look at the driver. The white-wall tires smoke and squeal as the powerful engine drags me back the way I just came. Seeing me bearing down on him like the hammer of God, my tail panics, turns rabbit. A lot closer to the mouth of the alley than me, the pick-up manages to back out into the street before I'm even halfway there. Through the passenger-side window, I just catch a glimpse of a white male face and over-styled blond pompadour behind the wheel before the Ford lays rubber and peels away into the night.

Canter's.

I park in the side lot, step over the bum that lies like a speed bump on the sidewalk out front, and shoulder my way through a pair of smudged glass doors.

I wave off the cute hostess who offers to seat me, and beeline it over to the pay phone. There I chase a quarter with a dime and hunt-and-peck out the number Vin gave me for Leroy Watkins.

He answers on the first ring, with a wary, "Who dis?"

"Leroy?"

"It's *Leh*-roy. *Leh*-roy. Get it straight, fool."

"Sorry, didn't realize you were French."

"French? I ain't no motherfuckin' French. I'm straight up red-blooded American, fool. Who is dis?"

"The name's Mick. Mick Angel. I got your number from a mutual friend. Vin Prince?"

"Yeah, so? Whatchoo want?"

"I was hoping maybe we could do some business."

"You want to do business? Man, I don't even know you. You

sound like a mufuckin' cop."

"I'm not a cop. I'm just a fella with some extra cash on his hands and no place to spend it. Vin thought maybe you could help me out."

Silence on the line, then. "Gimme your number, fool. I call you back after I talk to Vin."

"I'm at a pay phone. No number. How 'bout I call you back?"

"You ain't got no cell phone? Everyone got a cell phone."

"Not me."

A derisive puff of air like you hear during a glaucoma exam crosses the line. "A'ight, fine. Gimme ten minutes, fool."

"Right," I say, responding to the guy's natural salesmanship. I like him already.

We get off. I go sit at the counter and order a coffee—black— from the wrinkled blue-hair there.

"That's a smart-looking suit," she tells me as she pours it. "I wish more people of your generation dressed like you."

I smile at her. I'm probably old enough to have banged her mother. Hell, maybe I did. I thank her and drink my coffee and wait. Then I get up and go call Leroy back.

"Who dis?"

"Who do you think?"

"Don't get smart with me, mufucka. Who you think you be talkin' to?"

"All right, sorry. It's Mick again. So how 'bout it?"

"Yeah, you check out. Vin says you cool, you cool. You got a ride, Mr. No-cell-phone-having-mufucka, or you short one a them too?"

"I got a ride."

"A'ight, where you be at?"

"Fairfax. You?"

"Don't worry where I be at, fool. I'm rollin'. That all you need to know. That how I do."

I sigh. "Fine. Great. S'now what?"

"I'm busy right now. You be outside a diner called Dolores smoking a cigarette in ninety minutes. I'll roll by. If I like what I see, I'll pick yo' ass up. If I don't like what I see, I keep on rollin'."

"Fine. Where is it?"

"Sa-Mo Bouly, baby. Just west a the 405. Ninety minutes. Don't be late. Leh-roy don't like to wait."

I have some time to kill before meeting Leroy, so I head to the Blue Veil. If you've seen one strip club you've seen 'em all—streaked mirrors, loud music, greasy pole, flashing lights. The Blue Veil is no different—except maybe a little louder. And greasier.

The world behind the black glass doors is violently sexual. Except for the ever-shifting lights of the two dance stages the place is disturbingly dark in a way that you get the feeling is less about atmosphere and more about hiding the kind of stains that can only be seen with the help of a black light. The unmistakable scents of sweat and vanilla and menstruation fill the air. Semen too, but that goes without saying.

On the twin stages strippers stalk, crawl, and pace like caged wild animals, earning self-esteem a dollar at a time. The gawking men who ring them attempt to lure the predators to them with their stacks of ones, oblivious to the danger, until their wallets are attacked by ferocious bare tits and gaping g-string asses.

A sour-looking cocktail waitress with a face like an old catcher's mitt leads me to a tall, beer-sticky table at the back. She asks what I want to drink like she has a thousand more important things to be doing other than her job. I try to be understanding. With a face like that I'd be sour too. I order a Scotch. Single malt. On the rocks.

When she comes back with it, I fat tip her with a twenty; tell her to keep the change. She smiles at me now. She likes me now. We're good friends now.

"Let me ask you something," I say, making use of the good will I've purchased. "I haven't been here in a while, but I used to come in a lot and get dances from Dallas. She around tonight?"

"Just saw her. She's getting changed."

"Great. Would you tell her I'd like to see her?"

"Sure thing, hon," she says, favoring me with a lemon-pucker smile as she moves off.

Time in the Blue Veil passes like time in prison. I should know. I listen to songs I don't know and don't get; songs that sink under the screeching nails-on-a-chalkboard weight of guitars. I drink. I smoke. I wait and wait some more.

"You wanted to talk to me?"

I tear my eyes away from the topless Asian girl writhing on stage to find an attractive bleached blonde with cold eyes and a dissatisfied mouth that looks made to complain standing at my side. Her skin looks very tan against the paleness of her silk bra and panties. She smiles at me, but it seems forced, like a grumpy TV cat that has been trained to do tricks against its nature.

"You must be Dallas."

She nods, her face pretty despite its bitchiness. Or maybe because of it.

"Pull up a chair."

With a sly grin she reaches out and fingers my tie. "Let's discuss terms first."

"There are terms?"

She nods again. "I'm at work. I can't just sit around and talk all night. I'm here to make money."

"I get it. How much will it cost me?"

"Same as a lap dance. Twenty a song."

"Pretty steep just for a little conversation. I thought talk was supposed to be cheap."

She shrugs. "Inflation. You want cheap, talk to one of the other bitches."

I can't help but notice the way her huge fake breasts strain against the sheer material of her bra. Then again why would I want to? "All right, why don't we start with five songs." I peel off one of Reesa's hundreds and stick it to the table.

Dallas's eyes go wide at the size of my roll. I can almost hear her brain clacking like an abacus, wondering how much she might be able to get me to part with and for what. She peels the bill from the table with a crackle and makes it disappear into her D-cup like a master magician.

Rewarding me with another Frigidaire smile, she sits on the chair next to mine and I'm reminded of Reesa taking her stool the night before. Dallas suffers by comparison. Though lean and muscular, her body lacks the fluid grace of Reesa's soft curves. She looks gamey to me. Hard. For me, a night in the sack with her holds all the allure of a night spent humping a wooden post. A fella can get splinters that way.

"What's your name?" she asks.

I tell her. Then I say, "So let me guess—you're from Dallas, right?"

She shakes her head. "Fort Worth, but that didn't have the same ring to it."

I'm inclined to agree. She reaches out and traces one long fake nail along the outer rim of my ear. It's intended to be seductive, but it just makes me want to scratch.

"You're adorable, you know that?"

"I bet you say that to all the guys."

"I do." She shrugs. "But I mean it with you."

"You're gonna make me blush."

She smiles. "So you have something specific you wanna talk about, or will any topic do?"

"Something specific. Someone rather. Raya Van Cleef."

Her expression changes ever so slightly. She pales beneath the fake-bake stripper tan. The subtle scent of wariness fills the air. "Who?"

I take out the picture of Raya, flash it in front of those ice-water eyes. "I'm looking for this girl."

She shakes her head. "I've never seen her before."

The pungent scent of bullshit stings my nostrils. "Really? I was told you knew her."

"Who told you that?"

"A friend of hers."

"Well, whoever it is told you wrong. I don't know her."

"She didn't live with you?"

"What part of 'I don't know her' don't you understand?"

"I hear you saying it, problem is I don't believe you. I know you know her because the person who told me mentioned you by name. C'mon, spill it. What's it gonna take? More money? What's a gal like you charge for telling the truth? Dollar a word?"

I'm rewarded with the face behind the mask; the ugly, sneering one she tries to hide at work because men just don't pay hard-earned money to spend time with a face like that.

"Fuck you. This conversation's over, asshole." She stands.

"But I'm paid up through three more songs."

"Yeah, so sue me for it."

An amused smile on my face, I watch her move off, her hard-muscle hips moving like a metronome in silk panties.

9

I find a spot on Santa Monica Boulevard just out front of Dolores. I light a cigarette and lean against the Benz and wait until a black Lincoln Navigator rolls up on spinning silver rims. When the black-tinted window rolls down I get my first look at Leroy Watkins behind the wheel. I know him immediately from the fixed scowl set below a black dandelion puffball Afro that quivers on his head like a grouping of Daddy Long Legs spiders.

"You the fool who called me?"

"Good guess."

"You look like a mufuckin' cop. You lucky I stopped."

"I feel lucky."

"Get in, fool."

I tug the door open and climb aboard. Inside the truck seems big enough to warrant its own time zone. Beside me I see that Leroy is dressed head to toe like a full-fledged member of the Los Angeles Lakers. A short one. Mirrored window glides up.

Automatic locks thunk down. We pull away.

I smell the nervous perspiration of the second guy just before the black hole mouth of his Glock kisses my left temple, but not soon enough to stop it. My own gun might as well be at the bottom of a rain-gutter, for all the good it can do me tucked out of reach in my waistband at the small of my back.

The gun smells like it's been used recently. A fact I don't exactly find reassuring. I don't know if a bullet to the brain would kill me or not. Probably not. Probably it would only turn my brains to scrambled eggs and I'd live on as some sort of drooling immortal vegetable. That is if someone was kind enough to administer regular blood transfusions. In any case, I'd rather not find out.

In the truck's rearview, I can see the black-skinned gunman is every bit as bald as Leroy isn't.

"You gonna introduce me to your friend, Leroy?"

"No," Leroy says. "My boy, he don't like to meet mufuckas in case he gots to shoot mufuckas. Easier for him dat way."

I nod. "Makes sense."

Leroy hooks left and pulls into a space on a darkened, car-studded side street.

"Okay, pharmacy's open. Whatchoo want, fool? You name the drug, I got it. You look like a cat be into H to me." Got to give it to him, the guy knows his trade.

"I don't want drugs."

"Say what? I thought you wanted to do bidness. You better not be wastin' Leh-roy's time. For real."

"I do want to do business, only for information, not drugs.

I'm looking for a girl. Raya Van Cleef." I ease the girl's picture out and show it to him.

"Aw, hell no," Leroy says, turning to his boy. "You belee dis shit?"

"I know she contacted you," I continue, doing my best to seem unfazed by the gun currently tickling my temple. "I'm willing to pay for any information you can give me."

"I don't know what you heard, fool, but Leroy don't be givin' out no information to mufuckas. Belee dat."

"C'mon, you must know something. When's the last time you heard from her?"

"You mufuckin' hard a hearin', fool? I said I don't give out no information. Shit."

"C'mon. You're here. Might as well make some money."

"Mufucka, if I want yo' mufuckin' money I'll cap yo' dumb ass an' take it."

"All right, look. We can do this the easy way and you can walk away with a little money, or we can do it the hard way and you can walk away with a limp."

Leroy and his boy enjoy a cackle over this. I smile along with them and wait for the laughter to subside.

"Shee-it, white boy. I don't know if you be crazy or just stupid."

"Can't help ya there," I say. "So what's it gonna be?"

Leroy pretends to think, but I can smell the answer coming as large quantities of rage-smelling testosterone and adrenaline dump into his bloodstream and jet from his pores.

With a vampire's cat-quick reflexes, I simultaneously jerk my head out of the way, reach up, and snap the gunman's wrist, forcing the barrel back at Leroy even as he opens his mouth to give the order to shoot me. The gunman yelps like a kicked hound. The gun fires. The bullet slams home deep in Leroy's knee, giving him the limp I promised him. Call me old-fashioned, but I like to keep my promises.

My ears ring from the gunshot. The metallic sister-smells of blood and cordite fill the cab. Normally, the smell of all that fresh blood would act as a catalyst, sending me into a berserk feeding frenzy, but having an idea what I might be in for, I took precautions. I braced myself with a healthy fix after leaving the Blue Veil. As a result, I'm able to contain my blood lust.

Mere seconds have passed. In attack mode, a vampire experiences the world the way I imagine a fly must—with every other creature moving through space and time at an amusing snail-crawl pace. Leroy screams. His hands slo-mo to his exploded knee. The Glock falls with a leather-soft thud on the seat beside me. With my left elbow, I battering-ram baldy hard in the mouth. His eyes roll back. He spits teeth like watermelon seeds and sinks unconscious to the floorboards.

I turn to Leroy, who whimpers beside me. It seems the fight has gone out of him, but I pick the Glock up just in case.

"Aw shit. Lookit whatchoo done to me. Fuck!"

"You did it to yourself," I tell him. "Your choice, remember?"

"Fuck! I gotta get to a hospital, man."

"That's up to you too," I say. "The sooner you answer my questions the sooner you can go have that looked at."

"C'mon, man. I could bleed to def."

"That's the deal. Take it or leave it."

"Shit. Whatchoo wanna know?"

"Why doesn't anyone listen the first time 'round? The girl, Raya. Where is she?"

"I don't know."

"When's the last time you saw her?"

"I dunno. A few weeks ago. I took some crystal by the crib she be crashin' at."

I take my notepad out. "Gimme the address. The place you took the shard."

He gives it to me. From the number, I see the place falls in the seedy no-man's-land section where Hollywood starts its lingual and cultural transition to Koreatown.

"How many times did you go see her there?"

"I dunno. A few."

"What'd you think when you all of a sudden didn't hear from her any more?"

"Nuttin'. She's a speed-freak. They disappear all the time."

"You didn't hear anything about where she might've gone or what might've happened to her?"

"Man, I didn't hear shit, a'ight?"

A feverish sheen of sweat has broken out on Leroy's brow just below the 'fro. He's lost a fair amount of blood. He must be in a lot of pain. Can't say I feel too bad about it though.

I use the gun butt to knock him out, then pocket the ammo clip and check the chamber is empty, before tossing the Glock out of the window. I rifle Leroy's pockets and come out with a roll of hundreds that would gag a gimp. I pocket the cash too and start to go, but the lure of his blood is too much to resist.

I am running short after all. A little taste now will help get me through the drought.

Careful not to use my teeth, I bend and drink straight from the sucking knee-wound. I don't take too much. Just enough to take the straight-razor edge off my thirst. In return for the favor, I locate Leroy's cell phone, punch in nine-one-one, and hit send before I go. I figure it's the least I can do.

And the most.

10

The one-story house is guarded by a low, nincty-cight-pound-weakling chain-link fence, and has a glum look about it. Like every other house in the neighborhood, black iron bars protect the windows and doors. The white paint of the walls is cracked off in places, and the yard could use a good mowing, but it isn't the flophouse I was expecting. By the front door, a porch light burns like a lighthouse beacon.

It's late for visitors, but I step up onto the porch and knock anyway. No answer. I knock again, louder this time. Still nothing.

Stepping to the edge of the light, I look around for nosey neighbors. The neighborhood is quiet this time of night. Everyone seems to be in bed minding their own damn business. Good. Just the way I like it.

I go back to the Benz and grab a set of lock picks I keep taped up under the passenger seat for just this sort of thing. Then I go to work on the lock. There was a time when springing a lock like this would have been a cinch for me. No more. Locks are trickier now than they were in my day, and my numb and clumsy fingers have lost the subtle feel for the work. It's taking too long. I curse under my breath. Another thirty seconds and I better walk away if I know what's good for me. I hear a gentle click as the last pin tumbles. I'm in.

It's dark inside. I shut the door behind me hoping there isn't a deep-sleeping Rottweiler home. Doesn't seem to be. I don't smell one in any case.

I go in search of some sign of Raya. I don't bother to turn any lights on. Lights can give you away, and my vampire eyes allow me to see well enough in the dark without them.

The inside of the place is much like the outside. Not awful, but not real goddamn nice either. What furniture there is, is inexpensive and worn. Dishes sit unwashed in the sink. Opened bills addressed to someone by the name of Callie-Dean Merriweather are stacked on the kitchen counter. A pile of unfolded laundry waits on the couch. An ashtray full of lipstick-stained butts sits forgotten on a scarred coffee table. Washed nylons hang from the shower rod in the bathroom. But it's in the bedroom that I find the goods.

The old-fashioned cedar hope chest at the foot of the bed catches my attention right off. Not the chest so much as the fact that it has a lock. It seems like bad karma to lock your hopes and dreams away in the dark. That is, unless they're the kinds of hopes and dreams you don't want others to know about. It makes me curious. I pick the simple disc tumbler and fish around. Beneath a yellowed wedding dress and several mothball-stinking quilts I come across a photo album.

I take a seat at the edge of the bed and flip through. It's no family album. Inside I find page after page of snapshots of different teenaged kids who stare into the camera alongside a woman. There is something off about the shots; something subtly disquieting about the way the woman looks into the camera, as if she holds a dark and amusing secret only she knows, one she wants to share with herself when she looks back on these photos at some future point in time. I can't explain it any better than that, but somehow the whole thing gives me the heebie-jeebies. The fact that I recognize the woman only enhances the effect.

The very last picture in the book is of Raya; Raya with one skinny arm tossed around the shoulders of the woman and smiling a great big drug-induced Cheshire Cat smile. I peel up the cellophane and rip the photo from the black background where it has been glued. I tuck it away and poke around a little more. I find one more thing of interest. Then I go sit in darkness on the uncomfortable couch next to the pile of laundry and wait for the woman in the pictures—the one who looks so familiar—to come home.

Callie-Dean Merriweather of Fort Worth, Texas, arrives home a little after three in the A.M. She is different now from the girl I met in her skivvies earlier. First, in her faded denim asshuggers and baggy hooded sweatshirt, her face scrubbed free of makeup and hair pony-tailed at the back of her head, she looks more like a college co-ed than a stripper. I like her better like this. Second, she is wired. Evidently, between the time of our last meeting and now, Callie-Dean got her talons on some coke. I can see its effect in the way her too-alive eyes seem to want to pop free of her head. I can smell it in her system.

She isn't alone. A big, heavy-set lug with jowls and dark hooded eyes enters behind her. He has a plowshare nose and a free-on-leave smile. He wears a suit, indicating he went straight to the strip club from whatever convention he is in town attending. His tie is loosened, and he carries his suit jacket slung over one shoulder. It's supposed to make him look cocky and confident, but all it does is expose the dark sweat stains that spread like squid ink from his underarms. I can smell his alcohol-sour taint from the doorway. He's small-time and doesn't know it.

Callie-Dean tells the lug to make himself comfortable and shuts the door and flips a light on. They both freeze, seeing me making myself uncomfortable on the couch.

"'Bout time you got home, baby. I was gettin' worried."

She gasps. He scowls. I smile.

"What the fuck are you doing here?" Callie-Dean demands. There's the face I know and love.

"What can I say? I missed ya."

"Who's this? Your pimp?" the lug asks.

"Close," I say, standing now and moving over nearer them. "I'm her parole officer. I came by to make sure Callie-Dean hadn't gone back to turnin' tricks, but it looks like I'm too late. Gonna hafta make an official report about this. What's your name, fella?"

The lug goes all wobbly-kneed and scared-like. Probably

thinking of his wife and three kids back home in Smalltown, Nowheresville. "Hey, I just came by for a drink. That's all."

"Relax," Callie-Dean tells him. "He's not a parole officer. He's just a full-of-shit private investigator."

Unsure who to believe, the lug looks at me. I just shrug.

"Well anyway, it's pretty late," the guy says, pretending to check his watch. "I'd better get back to my hotel. Got early seminars tomorrow."

He starts to back toward the door, but Callie-Dean stops him by taking hold of one hairy-knuckled paw. She looks him in the eyes, doing a fair imitation of my hypnotic gaze. "Wait. You know all those things we discussed at the club? All the things you said you wanted to do to me? You can do them. For free. Every last little one. All you have to do is get rid of him first." She stabs her sharp little chin my way.

The lug looks over again, sizing me up. Now he's conflicted. I just shrug again, light a fresh smoke, and wait to see how it all shakes out.

The lug leans close to her, whispers, "Even the one thing? The thing I said I didn't have enough money for?"

Callie-Dean nods. "Okay, sure, but for that you gotta hurt him. I wanna hear something break." She speaks to him, but it's all for my benefit.

The lug nods, hands her his jacket, then puts his best mean-mug on and looks at me. "You heard the girl. You ain't supposed to be here. Time to go." He takes a step toward me, chest puffed out like a rooster in a cockfight. Somehow it seems appropriate. I stay put.

"You're making a mistake, buddy," I tell him. "You've been drinking. You're not thinkin' straight. A trashy two-bit hooker like her isn't worth all this. There's no percentage in it. On the one hand, you get a beating. On the other, you get a venereal disease. Either way it goes down, you lose. So why not just be smart, go back to your hotel and sleep it off, huh?"

"Get him, Tom," Callie-Dean says through clenched pearly-whites. "Tear his goddamn head off."

I can see that the thought of all the things she'll do that Tom's wife won't has his mind made up. I wait for him to make his move. When he does, I step in, meeting him halfway. Whatever it is Tom has in mind to do never gets done on account of my rearing back and smashing my forehead down hard into his nose. It breaks with a gristly pop. Blood jets from his nostrils like a blast from a twin-barrel shotgun. Tom clutches his splintered nose and collapses to the worn dust-ball carpet with a pathetic mewl.

Why is it no one ever takes good advice when it's offered?

The smell of his blood bellows a fire to life in my guts. Doing my best to ignore the unignorable, I bend, grab Tom by one fatty arm, and help him to his feet. "Let's go, Tom."

"Look what you did to me," he says in a little-boy mumble of disbelief as I lead him over to the door.

"That's right," I say. "No fun, but that's as good as it's gonna get around here for you. So if you don't want a second helping, I suggest you head on back to the hotel and forget you were ever here. How's that sound?"

Ten-dollar tie clamped to his nose in an attempt to shut off the bloodworks, Tom nods. Sounds good. Sounds real good in fact. I open the double doors for him and send him on his way with a friendly pat on the back.

When I lock the doors and turn back, Callie-Dean is gone.

I find her in the bedroom, tearing her pink cotton-candy bedding apart in search of something.

"Lookin' for this?" I ask, taking the black Beretta I found stashed between the mattress and box spring during my own search from the waistband of my pants and showing it to her.

Seeing I have her gun, Callie-Dean stops everything, her face tight and all the uglier for it. Then, in the blink of an eye, her whole demeanor changes as dramatically as a chameleon on a branch as she switches from one lethal weapon to the other she has at her disposal. She smiles seductively.

"You know you're pretty good," she tells me. "I like a man who can handle himself."

"Save it."

"No really. It's a big turn-on. I know I was a bitch before, but why don't you let me make it up to you?" Showing me how big and cute her eyes can be, Callie-Dean reaches down and pulls her sweatshirt off over her head in one fluid motion.

"Put that back on," I tell her, trying to keep my eyes where they belong.

"No," she says cutely, biting on a long fake fingernail. "Not 'til you fuck me."

"I don't think that'd be a good idea, baby," I say.

"I think it's a great idea," she says.

"I'm a little short on cash."

She reaches back and unfastens her brassiere from behind, letting it slide free down her long tan arms and drop to the floor. Bending forward, she takes her jeans off, sliding them down her muscular legs and simultaneously showing her implants off to best advantage. I lose the battle with my eyes and let them do what they do best. I have to admit whoever her surgeon is, he does good work.

"A girl doesn't have to make money to want to get laid."

"That's just a fringe benefit, huh?"

"I like money, but I like cock more," she says all breathy-like as she climbs hands and knees onto the bed and aims her hard little panty-clad walnut-cracker at me. "C'mere an' fuck me."

When I don't dive slobbering onto the bed after her, she looks back over one circular-saw shoulder blade in confusion.

"I'm not gonna fuck you," I say.

For the first time the expression on her face suggests she might be taking me seriously. "Why not? You're not a queer are you? I mean, you're good enough looking to be one, and the hat's a little gay, but I don't get that vibe."

"I'm not a queer."

"Then what's the problem?"

"The problem is I have a sneaking suspicion if I went to bed with you I'd wake up with a steak knife forget-me-not in my chest. Don't feel bad about it, you just aren't my type. I like my women less Black Widow Spider."

"You motherfucker!" she yells, turning and attacking like a scorpion. I catch her by the pincers and push her back against the pillows. She comes skittering at me again. I push her back again. We stare at each other, her eyes seething with hatred, mine indifferent. Standoff.

"What do you want?"

"I want to finish our conversation. I know you suggested I sue, but I'd just as soon settle out of court," I say. "Turn the radio on if you want. If you cooperate we should be able to keep this to three songs."

"Fuck you."

"You already tried that. Didn't work.

"Tell you what, you do your best impression of a lady and I'll show you what else I found besides the gun. How'd that be?"

Callie-Dean hate-stares me. Unfazed, I take the snapshot I found of Raya from my breast pocket and toss it onto the bed between us.

Her cold eyes glance down at it, then back up. "So what?"

"So it's funny, you tell me you don't know her, but here I am at Raya's last known address and it turns out to be yours. On top of that, I find a picture of the two of you together. Coincidences like that might lead someone to believe you knew her better than you let on."

All of a sudden self-conscious, she grabs a pillow and hugs it to her, hiding herself from me. "Maybe I did, but that doesn't mean I know what happened to her."

"Tell me what you do know." I nod at the photo album that still sits atop the oak dresser where I left it. "Start with that book there. Who are all those kids?"

"They're just kids I tried to help. Kids who needed a place

to stay for a while."

"Well, don't take this the wrong way, but you don't exactly strike me as the philanthropic type."

"Fuck you. You're a real asshole, you know that?"

I do, but I don't say so. "Alright, so convince me. Why the sudden goodwill and charity?"

"Because I know what it's like to be on the street. I've been there. It's no fucking fun."

"No, I don't guess it would be," I say. "How'd you meet her? The question catches her off guard. "Huh?"

"How did you and Raya come to meet?"

"At a club."

"What club?"

"The Tomb Room."

"You're into Goth bands?"

"Sometimes." She shrugs. "I'm into lotsa things."

"I bet they're into you too."

"Fuck you."

"If you were just trying to help her out, why'd you deny knowing her when I first asked?"

"Why should I help you? I don't know you."

"And the fact that I'm trying to locate a missing fourteen year-old girl doesn't buy me anything?"

"Not in my book."

"The girl has a family. They miss her."

"Well, maybe she doesn't miss them. You ever think of that? When you run away from something there's usually a good goddamn reason for it."

"Yeah? So why'd she run away from you?"

The ice-cold eyes that stare back at me are as lovely as they are murderous. "Fuck you," she says again, in case I somehow missed it the other times. "Get out."

I sigh. I can't think of anything else that might be gained by staying. I know whatever she's hiding is the key to all of this, but I'm not going to get it out of her tonight. Not like this. My options are limited. I haven't been invited so I can't use my powers, and because she's a dame, I can't get physical with her the way I would a man. Well, I suppose I could, but I don't do that with dames; not even ones like Callie-Dean who might actually benefit from it. Goes against the rules. Times like this I wish it didn't.

"Make you a deal: I'll go, but I'm taking this with me." I swap the picture on the bed for one of my business cards. "I'll give you 'til tomorrow night to give me a call and tell me what you know or I'm goin' to the cops with it and you can talk to them."

Her eyes shoot wooden stakes as I place the gun atop the photo album and turn to go.

"You're a real prick, you know that?"

I do, but I don't say so.

11

From the *Los Angeles Times*, Sunday December 12, 1943:

HOLLYWOOD PRODUCER FOUND DEAD
KILLERS BROUGHT TO JUSTICE

Less than twenty-four hours after film producer Roy
Mcardle was found beaten and murdered in his
Hollywood Hills home, police have two suspects in
custody. Police were tipped to the potential suspects
after a neighbor, alerted by the sound of gunfire,
witnessed a man and woman exiting Mcardle's home
late Saturday night. Thinking something seemed amiss,
the neighbor, who wishes to remain nameless, managed
to get a description of the mystery couple's car and a
partial plate number to give police.

According to authorities, the vehicle turned out to
be registered in the name of ex-jazz musician-turned-

dope fiend Michael Angel. When police arrived at the Venice beach home Angel shares with his wife, Coraline Desmond Angel, they found the murder weapon, drugs, and thirty grand in cash belonging to Mcardle.

Mcardle, a long-time Hollywood insider with a long list of western and gangster pictures to his credit, was known for his mistrust of banks and for keeping his money in an office wall safe. Officials speculate that the murder was the result of a robbery gone awry.

The couple will be arraigned downtown early Monday morning.

It didn't take the L.A.P.D. long to track us down after the shooting. Five uniformed officers battered the Venice Beach door down and rousted us just before five the next morning. The real crime was we never got to spend a thin dime of the money.

The interrogation was just like in the movies, except without all the witty banter and clever lines. Real cops are never that clever or witty. Still, they had a good case. They had a body with a .38 caliber bullet in it. They had a snub-nosed .38 registered to me that they believed had done the shooting. They had the eyewitness who saw a car, also registered to me, leaving the scene of the crime. They had the bag of money belonging to the victim found stashed under my bed along with the gun. As they put it—they had my ass on a platter. The only thing they didn't have was the right person fingered for the crime, but I couldn't see the point in arguing.

My main concern right then was for Coraline. A guy like me,

I figured, was ready-made for prison—hell, it was a wonder I'd avoided it that long—but a girl like Coraline couldn't hack it on the inside. With her enthusiasm for life, she would quickly blacken at the edges and die like a pressed flower between those gray walls. I couldn't have that on my conscience because when it came right down to it, I blamed myself for everything. None of it would have happened if I had loved her the way she deserved. If I had never let her try dope. Or if I'd stopped her from selling her body. Or if I'd gone to visit Roy alone. I could have changed things every step of the way and I hadn't done it. I'd let her down. I figured I owed her. So I took the rap.

I told the detectives all about how I'd forced Coraline to go along to the house and beat her up when she tried to refuse. I told them how I'd made her use her familiarity with Roy to get me inside. And how I'd killed him once I'd got hold of his money to keep him from squawking. They bought it; ate it up in fact. And why not? Dames with faces like Coraline's only did things like that in the movies. In the real world they got done by thugs with mugs like mine.

My trial began in April of 1944 and only took two weeks. It seemed about right to me, considering my confession and all the evidence the D.A. had gathered against me.

In exchange for a plea to a lesser charge and six months in a women's correctional institution, Coraline came and testified against me as the prosecution's star witness. Despite the circumstances, I was glad to see her. I spent those days memorizing every detail of her. The way she wore her black hair swept back from her face the way I liked best. The dimple in her right cheek that only appeared when she smiled. The dark freckle at the base of her neck. If I was going away—and it sure looked like I was—I was going to do my best to take her with me any way I could.

"I didn't want to go, but he—he made me. He hit me when I said no. I—I was scared. So I went. I went and I watched him shoot poor Roy dead."

She was a wonder on the stand. She cried on cue and told the sympathetic jury what a monster I was, how frightened she had been, how horribly scarred she was from the terrible ordeal, how sorry she was to have been involved in any way. By the end of her testimony, even I was half convinced I'd done it.

The vote was unanimous. Guilty. No surprise there. In fact, the only surprise of the whole trial came during the sentencing phase when it took jurors only twenty-eight minutes to decide to give me death. It was a record for that time.

As they lead me out past Coraline, I stared deep into those acetylene-torch eyes. The look in them was a violent twister of love and sorrow and relief. I stared until they pulled me out of that courtroom and I couldn't stare any more.

Then I went and waited to die.

Time on San Quentin's death row unfolds slowly. That would seem to be a good thing considering what awaits you at the end of the line, but it's not. Knowing what's coming only drives home the futility of the never-ending days. Days stacked on weeks stacked on months stacked on years like a house of cards and just as pointless.

All that time, I never heard so much as a single word from Coraline. Not a call. Not a letter. What I got was nothing and lots of it. I'm sure a lot of guys would have been sore about that, all things considered, but I didn't blame her any. I was glad of it, if you want to know the truth. I had not given up all I'd given up so she could waste her life pining for the dead. I wanted her to live. During the endless, countless hours of nothing to see and nothing to do, I created whole lives for her. I imagined her cleaned up and using her looks and talent working in the pictures, or traveling the world, seeing sights I'd never see, or raising a family with some average Joe who treated her like she hung the moon. You see, it didn't matter what to me, just so long as she was doing something with my sacrifice. Anything. It didn't seem much to ask.

I guess it was though.

Toward the end of 1945—November if I recall—I noticed a small article in the week-old copy of the *Times* I'd managed to get my hands on. The story explained how workers at the city dump had found the partially-nude body of a young woman. The body had later been identified as belonging to one Coraline Angel, the same Coraline Angel who had made the papers as an unwilling accomplice in the scandalous murder of producer Roy Mcardle. A heroin addict and prostitute, it was speculated that she had overdosed in one of the many east Los Angeles flophouses that had cropped up since the war and been disposed of by the other junkies hoping to avoid trouble with the law.

I must have read the story fifty times. A hundred. I just

couldn't seem to wrap my mind around the idea that Coraline was gone and it had all been for nothing. She hadn't done a good goddamn thing with the opportunity I gave her. Not a good goddamn thing. And if that was the case, then I was a sucker for doing it. Worse, I no longer had my hopes for her or my good thoughts about my one truly selfless act to get me through the days. I think I hated her for that most of all.

There was nothing left for me. The next day I got busy dying. I called my lawyers and demanded that they waive what remained of my appeals. It didn't take much convincing. The date was set and I looked forward to it like a kid does Christmas.

I only had a single visit my whole time on death row and it came the night before my scheduled execution. The warden himself appeared at the door to my cramped deathwatch cell to tell me.

"You've got a visitor, Angel."

I watched from my sheetless single bed as the door locks geared back and a habited nun entered my cell, eyes downcast, face veiled in shadow.

"Please leave us," she whispered to the warden.

"I don't think that's a good idea, Sister. This one's a killer."

She turned to him then, looked him in the eye. "Leave us."

"Leave… " he mumbled.

When he was gone, the door locked in place behind him, the nun turned to me and removed her coif and veil, and I found myself staring in shock at Coraline.

"Hello, lover."

Even in the dark, I could see she was every bit as lovely as I remembered—lovelier. But there were differences; stark and disturbing ones. Always full-bodied and healthy-looking even during her heaviest periods of heroin abuse, she appeared angular and sickly thin; her skin a canvas stretched tight across a bone frame. Her dark lustrous hair, which she had obsessively styled to perfection when I knew her, was a tangled mane framing a face of almost luminescent whiteness. Perhaps worst of all, the eyes that had always seemed to brim with life now had a weary intensity, as if some greater knowledge of secrets dark and arcane had worn her soul thin.

"You're dead. I read it in the paper."

"You can't believe everything you read, Mick."

She smiled, but it wasn't right. There was something off about her; something horrible and wrong. With the skittishness of a horse that scents a predator on the wind, I felt the sudden urge to bolt, but there was nowhere to go.

"I've missed you," she said, pulling me close.

I expected the embrace to feel as fragile as she looked, but the narrow arms that corralled me felt like steel bands. I wanted to shove her away, but I resisted the temptation with the thought that any sign of fear might cause those awful arms to slam closed around me with the crushing force of a bear trap and never let go. When she finally released me I felt like a fly jounced from the web of an approaching spider.

I guess it showed on my face because she said, "What's wrong? Aren't you happy to see me, baby?"

She tried to pout then, but that was another thing that had

changed. Coraline used to be a great pouter. World class. This was a sham. A fraud. As manufactured as a whore's orgasm. The new Coraline was a million miles past this sort of silly schoolgirl manipulation.

"I just can't believe you're here," I heard myself say.

"Of course I'm here. You don't really think I'd let them put the man I love to death without coming to see him one last time, do you?"

"That what you came to tell me? That you still love me?"

"Partly. I've always loved you, Mick. A lot of things have changed for me, but not that. But I have another reason too."

"Yeah, what's that?"

"You gave your life for me. I haven't forgotten that. I came to repay the favor."

"Yeah, and exactly how do you plan on doing that?"

"I can make it so they can't kill you."

"Let me guess—you have a stay of execution from the governor stashed in your brassiere."

"Why don't you check and see?" She took my hand and pressed it down the front of the habit. The joke was on me. She wasn't wearing a bra. Her breasts were strangely cool to the touch, but considering I hadn't had my hands within a hundred yards of a pair in three years I wasn't of a mind to be particular about it. Not even in her present state.

"That's not very nun-like of you."

"I'm afraid I'm not a very good nun. In fact, I'm not a nun at all."

"Yeah? What are ya then?"

Coraline transformed before my eyes. Her eyes grew black with blood and her fangs distended and her jaw unhinged. Nothing can prepare you for seeing the impossible; for the realization that the world is not what you thought it was. As I backed away in abject horror, I watched as her features melted back to perfection and Coraline once again stood before me. All except for her eyes, which remained black and awful.

"Jesus." I tried to think of a worse situation than being trapped with a monster in a locked high-security prison cell and found I couldn't come up with one.

"Sorry, baby. Didn't mean to startle you, but I didn't know how else to tell you. I'm a vampire, Mick."

"How?…"

"Look into my eyes. I'll show you," she said, seeming to glide across the space between us. Unable to resist, I felt myself drown in the murky depths of her black crystal-ball eyes.

It started with a call. It came from the butler of a wealthy Bel Air recluse by the name of Brasher. The butler told Coraline that his employer had heard rumors of her beauty and wished to meet her. It was late, but he offered to pay double her normal fee and to send a car for her, so she had gone. Of course she had.

Dressed in an ascot and smoking jacket, Brasher himself had met her at the door of his huge castle-like Bel Air home. He was a stooped, sickly, walking corpse of a man with yellow parchment for skin and a few spider's web filaments for hair.

"My dear, you are every bit as lovely as I was lead to believe."

He had just the slightest hint of a European accent, and used a stained white handkerchief to dab away the flecks of blood that collected on his withered lips as he spoke.

Seeing him, Coraline had second thoughts, but she was here now and she needed the money. Besides, what danger could this broken old man be to her? She'd gone in. Of course she had.

The house was dark and drafty. Blaming ancient wiring for the lack of electric lighting, Brasher escorted Coraline up a set of stairs and down a rat's maze of corridors by candlelight. They stopped at a study where a warm fire blazed.

Brasher directed Coraline to an antique divan and went to pour them each a snifter of brandy from the wet bar. Carrying her glass to her he said, "Tell me, my dear, do you enjoy games?"

"I suppose. Doesn't everyone?" Coraline asked, taking the snifter and tasting the brandy.

"Not everyone, no, but I enjoy them very much. I'd like to play one with you if you'd be so inclined."

"What sort of game?"

"A delicious one," he said with a death-rattle of a laugh. He began to say something else, but was interrupted by a disturbing fit of racking coughing. Coraline did her best to pretend not to notice the snarled clots of blood and mucus he caught in his handkerchief and hid away.

"I must apologize. I'm afraid my health isn't what it once was. What was I saying?"

"You were telling me about the game you wanted us to play."

"Oh yes. The game. Are you familiar with the children's game tag?"

Coraline looked at the old man, glass raised halfway to her mouth. "You want to play tag?"

"No. The game I have in mind is quite similar to tag however. The way it works is like this: this room will be your home base. So long as you remain in here no harm will befall you. Stay as long as you wish." A sweet smile on his lips, Brasher pointed to the door with one tree-root hand. "But the moment you step outside that door, the game is afoot. You try to escape from my house, and I'll try to stop you."

Brasher giggled.

"You're insane." Coraline set her drink down and moved for the door. But Brasher stepped in her way, grabbing her by her arms. Coraline tried to pull away, but to her amazement, he was much too strong for her.

"Let me go. I'm not playing any goddamn game with you."

"But, my dear, you're already playing."

Releasing her, he mutated into a vampire before her eyes.

Letting out a piercing scream of horror, Coraline fled the room, trailed by Brasher's maniacal laughter.

Coraline felt her way through the pitch-black halls, trying desperately to remember the route out, but lost her way. Terror-filled hours passed until she finally threw herself down in defeat, weeping distraughtly.

Brasher slipped up on her in silence. She never heard his approach. His first touch was as gentle as a lover's. Crouching by her, he nuzzled in darkness.

"You're it, my dear," he whispered.

***

When Coraline released me from the trance I found myself covered in a thin film of perspiration, crouched and shivering against the wall of my cell, just as if I had experienced the whole ordeal first hand.

"He raped me," she said. "He hurt me so bad, Mick. I felt him change while he was inside me. It went on forever. The longer it went on, the more violent he became, but he didn't bite me until, you know, until the end. And even then he didn't stop. He kept right on until he drank me all up."

"Jesus," I said, and that was all.

"He's a monster. Not all of us are, but he is. He needs to die. And if you still love me at all you'll come back with me and help me kill him."

Since the article I'd thought my love for Coraline was gone; dried up like a puddle in an arid desert heat. Despite the fear I felt, seeing her now I knew that was wrong. It had just changed forms. My love for her might have turned to steam, but I could still feel it hanging like humidity all around.

"Why go back at all? You're free. Safe."

Coraline shook her head. "You don't know him. He'll never let me go. He'll hunt me forever. As long as it takes. As long as he lives."

"I still don't see what you need me for. You're younger than he is. Stronger."

She shook her head. "Vampires get more powerful with age. It's hard to fool the one who made you. They know things about you. They can't read your mind exactly, but it's something like that. It's like they're able to read your intentions. If I came within fifty feet of him with a plan in mind to kill him he'd sense it."

"But I can do it, huh?"

"Yes, because I'll have made you. I won't lie to you, it'll be dangerous. But we could do it together. I know we could."

Reaching out, she took my hand. "What do you say, baby? You do this for me and I'll make it so they can't kill you tomorrow. Become like me, Mick. Then we can be together again. We could make it like it used to be."

"Uh-huh, except for the killing people for their blood part."

"Except for that," she said.

It was a story as old as mankind—young unhappy woman recruits a lover to do away with her old man, all for the promise of a new life together. Only this was the Nosferatu version.

"What do I have to do?"

She smiled again now. She was getting better with practice. "Just… invite me to stay… "

My fear and anger were overwhelmed by something more primal. My love for Coraline had always been a bitter pill. I didn't know if it was medicine or poison, but it was lodged in my throat and I was inclined to choke it down regardless. And besides, I wanted a second chance. Hell, I deserved one.

"You're invited."

She bent and kissed me with lips as soft and cold and red as refrigerated cherry gelatin. She moaned. Her fangs grew like twin erections around my probing tongue. Weak with love and sex and fear and death, I gave myself over to her and when the bite finally came it felt like the angry word of God.

12

Vin's place is gun-barrel dark when I get there. I decide to poke around anyway. Call it a hunch.

I enter the back way. The wrought-iron fence is just the way I left it: mangled. I slip through carrying my little doctor's bag. I jimmy the coved doors and step like a whisper inside. The place smells of spent meth.

I haven't been invited this time round. Too bad for Vin once is enough.

I find him sitting in darkness on the chaise lounge in the sunken living room. Even in the dark my night-vision eyes can see that he has been roughed up. His thin upper lip is swollen and one eye is puffy as a French pastry. His heartbeat is fast. I can smell the drugs in his system.

I scrape a match and light a smoke. Vin jerks like he's on wires and gasps and twists a light on, almost knocking it over in his hurry. He seems relieved when he sees it's me.

"Oh, it's you," he says.

"It's me," I agree.

"You scared the Christ outa me, guy. How'd you get in?"

I stab my butt doorward.

"Oh," he says, and blinks. He fumbles for a pair of Ray-Bans next to a glass pipe on the coffee table, puts them on. He seems to draw confidence from them. "What the fuck you doin' here anyway? You can't just waltz into somebody's house like this. That's called breaking and entering where I come from."

"Call it whatever you want," I say.

He stares. I stare. We stare. Vin decides to change the subject. "Leroy's lookin' for you, ya know that?"

"That who remodeled your face for you?"

Vin nods. "Yeah, Leroy and his fuckin' boy. What the hell were you thinkin', messin' with him?"

"He messed with me first."

"Yeah well, you pissed him off big time, guy. Big time. And you dragged me right in the shit with you. He was very, very majorly fuckin' pissed off that I gave you his number and vouched for you. I didn't want to do it, but I had to give you up to save my own ass."

"Well, I'm sure you held out as long as possible."

Vin sniffs, looks at the pipe, rules it out—for now. "Yeah. Yeah, sure, right. But they were serious, you know? Leroy's comin' for you. I mean, you shot his ass. Not that he prolly didn't deserve it, but he can't afford to just let somethin' like that go, ya know? He's got a rep to protect. I mean, fuck."

"Vin, shut up and look at me." He shuts up and looks. "I didn't come here to talk about Leroy."

"Well, what the fuck did you come to talk about?"

"Raya Van Cleef."

"Aw, Jesus. We already discussed all that. I told ya everything."

I give my head a shake. I blow smoke. "Not everything. Not about what happened between you two."

"The fuck you talkin' about?" He gives me the corner of his eyes behind the shades. It's funny, it seems the dumber people are, the less good they are at playing dumb.

"You know what. The last day. The day Reesa came home and found you and her little sister together."

"I don't know who the fuck you been talkin' to, guy, but that didn't happen."

The lie mixes with the remnants of the meth in the air, creating a smell as ugly as pedophilia.

"You raped a fourteen year-old girl, Vin."

He shakes his head big and exaggerated-like. "No."

"You did."

"Fuck you. I didn't rape no one. The little slut wanted it."

"That right?"

"Fuckin'-A it is. You don't know what it was like, her livin' with us."

"Why don't you tell me."

"She was always doin' shit to try and get me horny, ya know? Walkin' around in only a t-shirt and panties. Sitting too close on the couch. Leavin' her door open when she was changing. Shit like that."

"And I bet you just hated that."

"Look, I tried to stay away. But she threw it at me." The stink in the air tells me Vin isn't buying his own bullshit.

"Or maybe you were sick of all her teasing so you decided to teach her a lesson."

"Fuck you."

"I guess it doesn't really matter. Either way you're one sick son-of-a-bitch."

Vin sneers. It looks just like his smile. "Listen to you, all high an' mighty, but I bet if it'd been you insteada me, you'da done the same thing. The same goddamn thing."

"Ya think?"

"Fuckin'-A I do. Maybe she's a little young, but she was old enough to know what she was doing. Play with fire, you get burned. I mean, hell, we're only human right?"

I shake my head. "No, Vin, that's where you're wrong."

"The fuck you talkin' about?"

"I'm talking about the fact that I'm not human and, to be honest, I don't really think you make the grade either."

I stoop and unlatch the strap on my satchel. Vin watches, as if noticing it for the first time. "What's in there?"

"The vials I'm going to store your blood in," I tell him.

Vin's eyes get skittish the way someone's eyes do when they realize they might be all alone in a room with a crazy person. I smell a problem brewing. I take a step closer, but I'm too far away to stop his hand from darting into a crack between couch cushions and coming out holding a jumpy-looking nine-millimeter.

"What're you doin', Vin?"

"What I shoulda done the last fuckin' time you was here. You fucked up coming back, you know that?"

"All right, so I'll leave."

"I don't think so, guy. No one comes into my house and threatens me. You messed me up with Leroy. Messed me up good. This'll make it right." Vin racks the gun.

"You don't wanna do this," I say.

"Actually, I do." The meth makes him laugh too hard.

"What about the cops?"

He shrugs. "You broke into my house. I'm within my rights to shoot you."

"Just like that?"

"No. Just like this." He pulls the trigger. The gun barks. Twice. I'm too close to miss. The bullets catch me in the chest, spin me, and throw me back over a lounge chair. I go down. Hard.

I don't care who you are, bullets hurt. There's no getting around it. The pain isn't as bad as the first bullet I ever took— that was the worst—but it's far from good. Kind of like a root canal that starts before the Novocain has fully kicked in.

Vin's eight hundred dollar Italian shoes whisper sweet nothings on the carpet and then he's standing above me. "Thought you was a real tough customer, didn't you? Comin' in here and trying to intimidate me. But guess what, pal? Vin Prince don't intimidate."

I play possum, hoping maybe Vin won't shoot me any more if he thinks I'm dead. Well deader, anyway. He doesn't. What he does is rear back and kick me hard in the head like a forward trying to score on a penalty kick. I don't flinch. I don't move. I lie there and take it. If there's one thing vampires are good at, it's playing dead. Vin kicks me hard five or six more times.

"How'd you like that, you fuck? How'd you like that?"

I wait it out. I guess I sell it. Or maybe he just gets bored. Meth-heads need lots of stimulation. In any case, after two more half-hearted kicks, he struts back to the couch and sets the gun down in favor of his pipe.

I let him get a little medicine in him before I stand up and stagger over and tap him on the back of one shoulder. He turns with a yelp. I take the pipe and help him off with his sunglasses.

"Since you asked, I didn't like it, Vin. Not any of it," I say, feeling a sensation similar to a near-death adrenaline rush as the change begins.

Meth-eyed, he turns and goes for the gun, but it might as well be a feather duster for all the good it will do him now. I stop him with a vicious clamp to the throat. I squeeze until he gets all woozy and docile-like, then I set him back on the couch.

In my experience, there are two basic kinds of people—rabbits and deer. Rabbits bolt when they witness a vampire metamorphose. They'll Bugs Bunny through walls in the attempt to get away. They have to be caught and taken down. Deer, on the other hand, freeze up, hardly able to move or even breathe in the car-headlight horror of what they are seeing. There's never any way to predict who'll do what.

As it turns out, Vin's a deer. He sits on the couch, mouth open like a bulldozer blade, as he watches it happen. When it's done he just quivers and hyperventilates as I settle down beside him and take his head in my hands. Since it's his first time I try to make it nice, but I think it hurts him a little. The first time always hurts a little.

13

When I awaken, I go through the usual routine with Vin. I drag him to the tub. I sever what needs severing. I bleed him dry. I fill my vials. I erase evidence. I leave.

I take the fresh blood supply back to the office and store it in my mini-fridge where it'll keep. Then I strip my bullet-ruined shirt off and take a gander at my new ventilation system. They hurt, don't think they don't. The dime-sized holes at mid-chest level I can see, but I have to reach around and feel for the ones in back. Both bullets went all the way through. I'm glad about it. As glad as you can be about a thing like that, anyway. Good old Vin must have preferred solid bullets to hollow-points. I'm glad about that too.

I go to the deep freeze and grab a handful of the grave dirt that serves as my mattress. I drop it in a bowl and muddy it with some of Vin's blood. When I get the right consistency, I pack the holes finger-deep, spackle them off, bandage them, and wrap my torso in gauze. It'll take a little time, but they'll heal. The dirt and blood will speed the process. Vampire homeopathy 101.

Before I leave I put in a call to information to see if I can get an address for a Reesa Van Cleef. I can't. Somehow I knew it wasn't going to be that easy. I hang up. It rings as soon as the earpiece touches the cradle. I pick up.

"Angel."

"Jesus Christ, don't you ever answer your phone?" a female voice demands.

"I just did. Who is this?"

"Callie—Dallas. I've been calling you all day. Where have you been?"

"Went to a funeral. You ready to talk?"

"First you answer some questions for me and then, if I like the answers, maybe—just maybe—I'll talk."

"Sure. Ask away. Twenty a song seem fair?"

"Fuck you."

Enough sweet talk. "Okay, whatsit you wanna know?"

"I want to know what the fuck is going on. Who are you working for?"

"Raya's sister."

"That's bullshit."

"Yeah? What makes you think so?"

"I'm asking the questions."

"And you have a real knack for it," I say.

"Look, if I'm being set up, I'm not going down alone. I'll go to the cops. I'll make a deal. This whole thing didn't start with me and you know it."

"What whole thing?" Silence from her end. "Talk to me," I say. "It sounds like you're in over your head. Maybe I can help you."

"Yeah right," she sneers right through the phone. "You don't know the first goddamn thing about what's going on."

"You show me yours, I'll show you mine. Let's help each other. If you're in as deep as I think, you're gonna hafta trust somebody. Might as well be me. Whaddya say?"

"If you're fucking with me, so help me—"

"I'm not."

More silence. Then: "All right. All right, we'll talk, but not over the phone."

"Why not?"

"Because for all I know you could be recording this. Besides, I'm late for work. Come see me there. Late."

"How much will it cost me this time?"

"Fuck you."

I smile into the dial tone.

14

When it gets late enough, I take the back way down to the uninspired parking garage that serves my building. It is mostly deserted by this hour of night, being as I'm the only twenty-four hours a day resident. Off-white lighting clings like soap scum to the walls, making the place look even dingier than it already is. The Benz purrs with pleasure as I start her up. As I go to reverse, I see a familiar-looking black Navigator glide up behind me on blade tires and block me in. Great. Just what I need.

Leroy's boy jumps out of the driver's seat and comes rushing up, waving an equally familiar-looking Glock in my face with the hand that isn't in a cast. "Out the car, muthafucka. Let's go."

I get out and get a good look at him for the first time. I try to decide whether he's bigger than he is ugly, or uglier than he is big. In the end I take ugly by a nose; a bent, disjointed one. Not helping matters any is the fact that his lips are cut and swollen and six of his front teeth are broken or missing altogether. Evidently he hasn't had time to meet with a good goldsmith yet.

"What you lookin' at, bitch?" he asks, while we wait for Leroy to gather a pair of crutches together from the back of the truck and come join us.

"That pretty smile of yours," I say. "That natural or didja have work done?"

He puts the butt of the gun to work trying to erase my smile. It does the trick. I take a knee. I spit blood. When I get up I see that Leroy has crutched over and joined us.

"Look what the fuck you done did to me, mufucka," Leroy says by way of greeting.

"You ask me, you brought that on yourself."

"Oh I see—I axed to get shot, huh?"

"I gave you a choice. You picked the limp."

Leroy grins. "You a dead mufucka an' you don't even know it. Belee dat."

"I do believe it," I say. "Look, I've got some place to be right now, so how 'bout we continue this little reunion later, Leroy—"

"*Leh*-roy."

"Whatever. Here's your new choice: leave right now and keep sucking air, or stick around and quit cold-turkey."

"Naw, naw, you ain't givin' the mufuckin' choices dis time, fool. Leh-roy be givin' the choices. Belee dat. See—see first I gone have my boy shoot you in the leg, give your bitch-ass a chance to see how dat feel. Then, I give you yo' choice if you want the next one in the mufuckin' face, or the mufuckin' chest."

"'Preciate that," I say. "How 'bout the face? I've already taken two in the chest tonight."

"You think I'm mufuckin' playin' wit you, fool? You think dis here some kinda mufuckin' joke?'"

"No. You'd have to have a sense of humor for that."

Leroy looks over at Ugly. I can smell the rage in his system. "Shoot him in da leg, dawg."

Figuring I've been shot enough for one night, I give Ugly the eye and say, "Point the gun at Leroy."

Ugly's eyes ice over and he slowly pivots the gun so that it's pointing past me at his boss. It's fair to say that Leroy is more than a little flabbergasted by this development. Can't say I blame him.

"Aw no you ain't. I know you ain't pointin' that mufuckin' gun at me. You musta lost yo' mind, fool. The fuck you be thinkin'?'"

"Last chance, Leroy. You can still limp away from this."

Leroy ignores me. He only has eyes for his traitorous pal. "You my bitch, bitch. I'm tellin' you right the fuck now, you best get that gun outa my mufuckin' face."

The gun wavers ever so slightly. Got to give it to Leroy, he wields a lot of control. Too bad for him it's no match for my hypnotic gaze.

I lean close to Ugly and whisper in one soup-bowl ear. I have to get up on tiptoes to do it. "Keep the gun on Leroy. Don't let him move. Anything he tells you to do to me, you do to him. I'm gonna go move the truck. Nod if you understand."

Ugly nods. I head for the Navigator.

"Where the fuck you think you be goin', fool?" Leroy asks.

When I don't answer he turns back to Ugly. "I be tellin' you for the last time. Get dat gun off me and shoot that mufucka in the leg!"

The Glock fires with the Navigator's engine. Together the clap of the gun and the rumble of the engine sound like summer thunder in the garage. I look out the passenger side window to see Leroy collapsed amid his crutches at the side of the Benz, a fresh bullet wound just above the knee in his one remaining good leg.

I move the truck. When I get back to the Benz, Leroy is sitting up clutching his leg, in the middle of an angry tirade. Can't say I blame him.

"What the fuck? You mufuckin' shot me, bitch! What the fuck you be thinkin'? Fuck!"

His boy doesn't answer on account of he is still under my control, but Leroy doesn't know it. Ignoring all the bleeding and yelling, I climb into the Mercedes and start her up.

"Mufucka's gettin' away, bitch. Shoot him. Shoot him right mufuckin' n—"

Blam! Leroy takes another bullet. In the shoulder this time. It drives him down hard on his back to the oil-stained floor like a tackle from a linebacker. It's no more than he deserves, but I don't feel good about it.

"Fuuuuuuuck!"

Much as I'd like to stick around and have a midnight snack, the gun was too loud. People will have heard. The cops will be coming.

Time to go.

I crank the window down so I can give Ugly one last instruction. "Help your friend," I say. I figure it's the least I can do.

And the most.

15

I drive east to the Blue Veil. It's been a long night, but I still intend to find out what Callie-Dean knows about all this, even if it means being less of a gentleman than I would prefer. But I'll leave that up to her.

When I get there, I locate my favorite mitt-faced waitress, who tells me that Dallas hasn't shown up for her shift. No call. No nothing. With a bad feeling rolling around in my stomach like two greasy ten-pound bowling balls, I leave and drive to Callie-Dean's house as fast as the Roadster will take me. I park on the street. The house is dark and sullen behind the chain-link. Not even a porch light burns tonight.

I get out, walk up, try the door. It is unlocked. Not a good sign. I take my gun out and turn the knob and shoulder it open. It opens like a mouth; the darkness inside illuminated by my night-vision eyes.

Everything looks exactly as I left it until I get to the bedroom. I smell her before I see her. Callie-Dean lies naked and lifeless

145

atop the pink cotton-candy covers, her eyes staring into the nevermore. Blood and brains create a grisly Jackson Pollock on the headboard behind her. The nine-millimeter hole in her forehead looks like a peephole into hell.

I look for the gun. I don't find it. Because suicides can't dispose of guns I rule that out as a possibility. It's thinking like that that makes me so good at what I do. The girl was killed. The question is why? And by who?

I nose around. I find her cell phone tucked beneath one blood-saturated pillow. I fool with the tiny goddamn buttons until I figure out how to get into her dialed call log. According to the log, the last call she ever made was the one to me.

Swell. Now I've got trouble. It doesn't take a genius to realize that once the cops discover her body, it'll only be a matter of time before they check her call log and then stop by my place with their sneaky cop questions. I make a mental note to purge my place as soon as I get home. The last thing I need is for them to decide to search and find vials of blood linking me to Vin Prince or any of the others.

There's nothing else for me here. The blood still in Callie-Dean's body will have gone bad as rancid milk by now and be just as useless to me. Damn shame. I pocket the phone, planning to dispose of it on the way home; no sense making it any easier for the cops to find me than it will already be. I close Callie-Dean's accusatory eyes and leave her the way I left her the night before—except more dead.

I smoke and drive. I ditch the cell in a rain gutter. My watch tells me it's going on one-forty-five in the A.M. I've been so busy tonight I haven't had any more time to try to figure out where Reesa lives.

I head to the Tropicana. I get there too late. Closed. Looks like this lover boy is out of luck.

I turn and head back along Melrose to the Benz when I see her trumpet player—a short, soft, bald egg of a guy—exit a side door and carry his case over to a dark sedan which sits in a side lot.

I detour. I slip up vampire-quiet behind him, clap a cold hand on one round shoulder. He starts, turns toward me, raising the black trumpet case as if for protection.

"Sorry. Didn't mean to startle ya," I lie.

"That's all right, buddy. What can I do for ya?" His eyes are wary.

"I'm a friend of Reesa's. I'm supposed to meet her tonight, but I don't have her address." It's no good. I sound like a stalker, even to me.

"You crazy? I don't know you. I'm not giving you her address."

"Okay, but just so we're clear: you know it, you're just not going to give it to me. That right?"

"Yeah. That's right."

Good enough. I move up close, throw an arm around him like we're old friends just in case anyone's looking, and jab my gun into the soft-boiled fat of his belly.

"Any way my friend here could convince you to change your mind about that?" I ask, my eyes selling near-death experience for all they're worth. "I mean, you don't really want to die tonight, do ya, pal? Not over something as stupid as an address..."

He sucks in a breath, pisses himself a little, jitters the address to me. A condo in Westwood. Wilshire Corridor. Upscale. She must be doing well to afford a place like that.

I thank him and give him the gaze and tell him to kindly disremember the conversation. He assures me he will. I start to leave, but then—not sure exactly why—turn back and tell him to hand the trumpet over while he's at it. He does it, easy as you please. I take it and walk away fast.

It feels good under my arm after all these years.

16

I get to Reesa's building a little before two-thirty. Twenty-three stories of pristine white stucco standing in wait to try its chances against the next big quake. I park at a metered spot up the street. I pull my kit from beneath the seat. I fix.

While I drowse, I dreamily open the black case and take the trumpet out. She's a knock-out. Her white polished brass gleams like a silk camisole in the streetlight. I hold her. I fiddle with her pearl-white buttons. I even put her to my mouth. We kiss, short and chaste, and then I put her back without playing a single note. Not on the first date. It's too soon for that. She wouldn't respect me in the morning if I did.

I get out and go see Reesa up on the thirteenth floor.

"It's late—" she says when she opens the door. She has on a black silk kimono tonight that matches her mood.

"I know. Sorry. Got a little busy with the case."

"You could've at least called."

"You're right. You want me to go?"

"I didn't say that, but if I let you in you're going to have to make it up to me."

"That right?"

"Mmm-hmm. And it won't be easy either. Could take all night."

"Well I'm a hard worker."

"You'd better be." She grins now, dropping the act and throwing her arms around me. We kiss right there in the hall. It's like the first time only more familiar. Hungrier. Better.

I let her take me by the hand and pull me inside and shut the door. I look around. The place is dim and neat. Minimalist. Very L.A. feng shui. A low table sits in front of an expensive cherry-wood futon, a bonsai at its center. High-heeled shoes and assorted sneakers mingle on a reed mat just inside the door. Oriental dragon paintings cover the walls. A fat Buddha leers knowingly at me from beside the fireplace. Candle-lit paper lamps flicker light around the room. It reminds me of an opium dream. Reesa bends at the knee in the manner of a Japanese wife and removes first one of my shoes and then the other. She looks up at me as she places them on the reed mat next to hers.

"Drink?"

"Maybe later," I say.

She stands with a grin and leads me across a red and black and white oriental carpet to a bedroom, hidden behind a pair of black-slatted rice-paper doors.

The room is dark, only lit by candles. We kiss at the edge of the bed. Careful of my wounds, I shrug out of my jacket and start to unbutton my shirt, but she pushes my hands away and does it for me. She stops, seeing the gauze straightjacket around my torso.

"What happened?"

"Bad paper cut," I say.

It earns me a smile. "Oh, tough guy, huh?"

I shrug.

"Well you should be more careful opening envelopes."

"Good advice."

"So you're okay?"

"I'll live," I lie.

"Can you—I mean, do you still want to?"

"Sure. Just so long as you're gentle."

"I make no promises," she says, pushing me down onto the embroidered comforter with a mischievous grin.

I watch her make the kimono disappear into shadows and I know that somewhere God exists. She comes to me, gentling in between my legs. She stares down at me, red locks hanging in her face. The unread contract sits between us again. This time I pick up the pen and sign my name.

In blood.

Afterward, we lay in a tangle of bed sheets and limbs. The smell of spent passion hangs like cordite in the air. It hasn't been like this for a long time.

Hell, maybe it's never been like this.

"You're amazing," she says breathlessly as I roll off of her slick and hungry flesh for the fifth time. "I've never met a man who could keep up with me. I mean, even on coke or meth, all the guys I've been with have needed to rest in between. How do you do it? Are you using tantra?"

"Something like that," I say. I could tell her that as a vampire I have some control over where the blood in my body goes, but I don't. I feel her shiver against me and reach down to pull the rumpled comforter over us. "Cold?"

"Just a chill. It's strange. Even after all that, your skin is so cool to the touch. Cold almost."

Her words snap me back to reality, reminding me of all the myriad reasons this will never work out between us. It also reminds me of another thirst that will soon need quenching.

"Let's go again," she whispers in the dark, rolling over and reaching down for me.

Feeling the approaching sunrise counting down like a time-bomb inside me, I gently set her grasping hand aside. "Can't," I say. "Time's up. Gotta go."

She gives me a disappointed "No," then a "How come?"

I stand and play a game of hide-and-go-seek with my clothing. "I won't lie to ya, doll. The truth is if I'm not home by dawn, well, I'll turn into a pumpkin." Reesa giggles. "You wouldn't want that, would you?"

She shakes her head like a little girl. "No."

I pull my pants on. Propped on one arm, she watches me. "So was this just a—you know—a one-time thing?"

"Weren't you counting? It was a five-time thing."

She laughs again. "You know what I mean."

"You tell me."

"I'd rather it wasn't."

"I guess I'd rather that too." I mean it, even though I know all this has us on the dead-end express straight to Nowheresville.

"Good." Looking tired-eyed now, she bites the head off a yawn and says, "Maybe next time we can try your freezer out."

"You wouldn't like it."

"Oh I dunno. Might be kinky." She gives me that too-cute smile as I shrug into my jacket with a wince.

I tell her we try doing what we did tonight in there and the only kinks she gets will be in her neck. Then I bend and kiss her goodbye and leave her smiling in the dark.

17

Gas as a form of execution was first conceived by a toxicologist by the name of Dr. Allen McLean Hamilton. The initial idea was to simply gas condemned inmates while the poor dumb bastards slept in their cells. When that didn't prove workable, the sadistic powers-that-be settled on the gas chamber. Seen by some as more humane than shooting, hanging, or electrocution, the idea caught on. It became the main form of execution for San Quentin penitentiary in 1938.

Kept hidden away in the prison basement like a shameful family secret, the San Quentin gas chamber looks like what it is: a death room. No way anyone would mistake it for a sauna. Just the sight of its octagonal six-by-eight witch-skin green metal walls is enough to make you go all weak in the knees. You enter it through an airtight oval door—the kind you see on submarines. The first thing you notice going in is that there are two chairs instead of just one, presumably in case the warden should find himself in a Noah's Ark kind of killing mood. Through five large square windows, stone-faced witnesses watch as the guards belt you into the chair with worn leather straps.

You wonder how many others the straps have been used on. You wonder if they fought. You wonder if you should. Something just doesn't seem quite right about going without a fight. But you don't. There's no point. Fighting makes about as much sense as jumping off a cliff and flapping your arms on your way down. So you don't. You let them. You let them belt you in. You let them do all the things they need to do to make you dead.

Glimpsed through perforations in the seat beneath you is a metal bowl. It holds a mixture of sulphuric acid and distilled water. Above it, a pound of sodium cyanide pellets hang in a gauze bag like a condemned man.

When the guards are done with their ministrations, they exit the way they came. You sense how goddamn glad they feel to be getting out of there. How glad they are they aren't you. The rubber sealed steel door shuts with a nasty vacuum-packed whisper. A clang would be more welcome. A large locking wheel seals you in like Amontillado in his cask, and all there is left to do is wait. So you wait.

Pretty soon the bag of pellets splashes into the bowl and the acid water and cyanide mix to create tendrils of hydrogen cyanide gas that crawl up to you like ivy through the perforations in the chair. You know you're about to die, but somehow you don't really, can't really believe it.

They've advised you that it's in your best interest to breath deeply from the start. Get it over quick. Shorten your suffering. But you don't. Maybe you didn't fight, but goddamn if you're going to just suck it in like fresh air on a breezy summer day. So you hold your breath. You hold it despite the burning napalm kiss of the gas on your skin. You hold it even as your closed eyes sting and tear. Even though it makes no sense and there's no goddamn point.

You hold it.

Until your lungs are bursting and you can't anymore. And then you suck a lungful of hellfire and brimstone and then the real horror begins. Like a sucker punch to the gut, your ability to breathe is cut off with that first breath. It hurts. Goddamn it hurts as it burns you from the inside out. But it doesn't kill you. Doesn't even put you under. What it does is cause something called hypoxia, which is just a five-dollar way of saying it cuts off oxygen to the brain. Hanging or shooting would be faster but those aren't options. Not humane enough. So, wide awake, lungs on fire, you asphyxiate. Every muscle in your body contracting and convulsing to beat the band as the toxin invades your bloodstream and your veins ignite like fuses on powder kegs. Wide awake, fighting for one more breath that never comes, you die.

The state of California put me to death at ten A.M. on March 14, 1946. No one claimed the body. No one came to the funeral service. They buried me six feet deep in the prison cemetery in a pine-wood coffin. I was thirty-three years old.

Becoming a vampire isn't like they make out in the pictures.

The pictures make it seem like you get bitten and alakazam—instant vampire. Wrong. Dead wrong. The way it really works is like this: first you get bit, which transmits the infection, then you become a carrier until whatever point you die, then, depending on how long you've been a carrier, there is a gestation period of complete unawareness, and then slowly, gradually, like a newborn infant, you begin to become aware of the world around you. The subtle light in the darkness. The smell of damp earth and your own decay. The cramped confines of your pine-coffin womb. And of course, an ever-growing, ungodly, unimaginable thirst. It's the thirst, building like pressure in a teakettle inside you, that ultimately compels you to break free of the grave and rise and hunt.

Scared and confused, I rose three months after my death like Jesus from his tomb. Free, I collapsed on the ground beside my grave, weak as a newborn foal, to find that the whole world had changed while I'd been away.

Or maybe it was just me.

Though my sense of touch was now deadened with unsettling leprotic numbness, each of my other senses had become a hundred times keener. A thousand. Thick clouds obscured the moon, making the night black, but a new-found infrared vision allowed me to see despite this. I could hear the beating hearts of life all around me. I could smell the blood pumping through arteries and veins. I was aware of the world in a new and predatory way. Every living thing seemed mine for the killing.

I smelled her before I saw or heard her. The stink of her sweet decay filled my nose as she materialized from the low-laying fog that had settled around the cheap, state-funded headstones.

Coraline.

"Hello, lover."

Her voice came from behind and carried a corpse-cold smile in it. I turned my head to look, but because of the cloud cover and her lack of body heat, she appeared as a dead spot in my infrared world. Like a black hole, I could only tell she was there by the lack of light that formed the shape of her.

I tried to sit up, but my atrophied arms buckled under me, and to my embarrassment, I found myself face down in the dirt again. Coraline came to me then, cooing like a new mother.

"It's okay, baby. Don't struggle. You're weak. That's normal."

She settled down beside me and propped my head in her lap and brushed crumbles of sandy dirt from the cheap suit the state had buried me in with one bone-cold hand.

"Don't you worry, darling, your Coraline is here now. I'll take care of everything."

"What have you done to me?" My voice sounded like it had been passed through a cheese grater.

"Nothing you didn't want me to. They were going to kill you, Mick. You didn't want that and neither did I, so I made you immortal."

"You made me a monster."

She shrugged. "Semantics."

Her nonchalance made me feel sore—real sore, if you want to know the truth—and if I'd been stronger, I might have hit her then. I don't believe in hitting women as a rule, but then

Coraline no longer qualified. She had become something else. Something dark and predatory. Something awful.

So was I.

"Anyway, baby, what's done is done. This is how it is. We have to focus on the future. We have a lot to discuss, you and I, but first you need your strength and for that you have to feed. You are thirsty, aren't you?"

I said nothing; just stared up into the void. Above, a cloud drifted and a cat's-eye moon winked through, affording me a glimpse of Coraline's face. She smiled down at me, as beautiful dead as she ever was alive. More.

As I watched, she lifted her shirt and exposed her full round breasts to the chill night air.

"What are you doing?"

"You're my baby bird," she said. "I'm going to feed you until you're strong enough to feed yourself. After all, a growing boy needs to eat."

Bringing one erect nipple to her mouth, Coraline bit into it with one crescent-moon fang and squeezed it to make the blood flow. Then, a maternal smile on her face, she pulled my head to her and gently pressed her cold, blood-slick breast to my lips.

The idea of drinking blood, especially her blood, and in this way, revolted me. I couldn't do it. I wouldn't. But in the end, the irresistible smell of blood and my own voracious thirst won out. They always do. And she was right; after all, a growing boy needs to eat.

***

Coraline took me back to the room she had taken at a fleabag motel, just up the road from the prison, where the visiting family members of inmates often stayed.

Upon checking in, she had used the coercive power of her own hypnotic gaze to impress upon the night manager her fervent desire that absolutely no one enter the room for any reason for the duration of her stay. He had agreed to see to it no one would, and had even chivalrously offered to move the oversized oak steamer trunk she had brought along into the room for her.

We spent the next few days dead to the world in that trunk, and the nights in a lustful Gordian tangle in the bed. Though our lovemaking was different now, newly tinged with darkness and blood and violence, it was every bit as passionate as I remembered. Though I hated to admit it, it felt good to be back in her arms. It was like nothing else mattered. Maybe nothing else ever had.

We holed up in the room until I was strong enough to travel and then we started back up the coast to the City of Angels. To Brasher and the nightmare that awaited.

Coraline had taken care of everything just like always. While waiting for me to rise, she had rented a Spanish-style bungalow only a few short blocks from the Venice neighborhood where we'd spent our early days together. She even equipped the joint with all the comforts of home: blacked-over windows, a refrigerator for storing blood, and a large, comfortable padded coffin. Over the next two weeks she came to me while she was supposed to be out hunting for Brasher. It was almost like old times.

Almost.

Our nights were spent making love and planning murder. We decided I should kill Brasher while she was supposedly away on a long-distance hunt. That way he wouldn't expect anything, and she wouldn't be around to give anything away should he attempt to probe her mind. According to Coraline, Brasher's butler and driver were under strict orders to vacate the property each day by dusk so that he wouldn't be tempted to feed on his hired help when he rose. As a result, the huge house would be empty except for the two of us.

Coraline had thought of everything. One night, a fresh bout of dark lovemaking behind us, she laid out the plan for me as we lay naked on the bed licking our wounds.

"It's always the same. He makes me lock a victim away in his study every night. When he rises, he goes in there and feeds first thing. He'll be drowsy after, so that's when you do it."

I objected, saying that it seemed low-down and dirty to kill a fella—even a monster like Brasher—in his sleep, but Coraline told me it was the only way.

"He's old, Mick, but he's powerful. Don't underestimate him. If you drop your guard, even for an instant, he'll kill you. Believe that."

Seeing the fear in her graveyard eyes where there should be none, I did believe it. She was terrified of him.

"All right," I said.

Naked against the rickety headboard of the bed, Coraline

reached out and grabbed the rumpled pack of cigarettes from the nightstand, lit one.

"The key is in the timing, but if we get it right it should be simple. Just wait until he's drowsing, then go in and shoot him full of holes."

"I didn't think bullets had much effect on vampires."

"They don't. Unless they're made of silver. All undead creatures are allergic to it. It won't kill him, but it'll hurt like hell and give you the advantage."

Smiling a crafty smile, she blew a ribbon of smoke that settled like fog around her boneyard tan.

"Okay, I shoot him. Then what?"

"Then, when he's wounded, you use the stake. Jam it through his heart."

"And that'll kill him?"

"No, but it will paralyze him as long as it's in there. He'll be completely incapacitated. Won't even be able to speak."

"Fine. Good. But how do I kill him?"

"You have to burn him," she said.

"It's the only way to be sure," she said.

I went to kill Brasher on a warm evening in June. I left Coraline at the Venice house to await my return. The scent of Honeysuckle filtered in through the open windows of the car as I drove up Sunset toward Bel Air, but all I could smell was blood.

I parked on a squirming Bel Air road and climbed a brick wall covered with thorns and brambles to get at the house.

From the shadowed canopy of a jacaranda tree, I lit a smoke and sized up the joint. With its high, ivy-covered walls and irregular stonework façade, it reminded me of a European castle. The arched front door was set back in a recessed alcove. Beside it, a sconce porch light burned invitingly, as if to say I was expected.

According to Coraline, Wilhelm Brasheer was a Hungarian aristocrat with ties to the old country. He had come over to America after being run out of France during the French Revolution. Forced to choose between his fortune and his head, he had wisely left the money behind. Why not? Money comes easy to vampires. What you don't earn you can always take, which is exactly what Brasher did.

After changing his name to the more American-sounding William Brasher, he had kicked around the east coast for a while before eventually migrating west to take part in the rough-and-tumble early days of the California gold rush. The story goes that after Brasher's arrival in early 1850, several Forty-niners with claims to large ore-bearing mines mysteriously disappeared. Stranger still, they had sold their claims to Brasher for pennies on the dollar just prior to their disappearances. Questions were asked, but not too many. Brasher had an uncanny ability to talk his way out of trouble, and after all, the papers for the claims were signed and legal. Amassing a fortune that far exceeded what he had left behind in Europe, Brasher had later moved to southern California and never left. The guy sounded like a real charmer. I couldn't wait to meet him.

I scuffed my smoke out on the flagstone drive and checked the load on the gun for the umpteenth time. Satisfied the bullets hadn't gone anywhere while I wasn't looking, I skulked around the side to the darkened service entrance and went in.

The place was dark and corrupt with the stink of decay. Brasher was an old vampire from the time before electric freezers. He slept in only a coffin and the whole place smelled of rot as a result.

Looking around, I found myself standing in a large empty pantry off a large kitchen. The kitchen didn't look like it got used much, but then why would it? Brasher always ordered out.

I shut the door behind me and listened hard. I got an earful of nothing for my trouble. Fighting the urge to check the load again, I moved into a long wooden hall that led past a formal dining room and stopped at a narrow staircase. I listened again. Still nothing. I thought back on the floor plan Coraline had insisted I memorize. The study was at the far back of the house on the second floor. The stairs would take me there. I started up.

The unmistakable scent of fresh blood assaulted me as I stepped into the upstairs hall. Coraline had fed me well before I left, but the overpowering scent stirred the need to change and feed deep within me. I felt it coil in my gut and press for release. So far, since being turned, I had managed to avoid a full metamorphosis into my vampire state. I had come close a couple of times while feeding, but had always managed to hold back. I was a little scared of it. More than a little, if you want to know the truth. I told myself that what I feared was the idea of giving up control and turning into some kind of mindless killing machine, but honestly I was more scared of how much I secretly wanted to let go, how much some new and horrible part of me wanted me to do exactly that.

I swallowed hard and shook my head to clear it. It worked, but only a little. I knew this was just the beginning. The longer I was exposed to the smell, the worse the need would grow and the more whatever it was inside me that wanted out would begin to rage against its restraints. It made me think of a shackled madman screaming for release from his padded cell. I had to keep my head about me. I needed to be able to think if I was going to succeed against a vampire as powerful as Brasher.

Time to do this.

Less cautious than before, I followed my gun barrel along the uneven wooden floors of the hall. With every step the smell of blood grew stronger, and with it, my desire to change.

The hall hooked right and so did I. Just ahead, light escaped from a thin crack at the base of a sturdy oak door. I moved to it. The intense smell of blood here told me that there was a fresh corpse somewhere behind it. If things were going as anticipated, Brasher would be there too, passed out unconscious over his last supper.

I took a deep breath and shook my head again like a driver fighting to stay awake at the wheel. Then I cocked the gun and turned the knob and stepped through.

The room was an abattoir. Rivulets of wet blood ran down the walls and puddled on the floor. Furniture and lamps had been overturned as if a life-and-death struggle had taken place. It had. On the hearth near the large fireplace lay the eviscerated body of a kid of no more than fifteen or sixteen. It was all just about as expected. There was only one thing missing from the scenario. Brasher.

I knew I should get out. I needed some time to recoup and come up with a plan B for finding and killing Brasher, but the lure of all that blood was irresistible. Maybe I could just have a taste. What would it hurt? The kid was already dead. Whatever use he might once have had for that sweet red nectar no longer applied. I'd just have myself a little taste. Not enough to make me sleepy. Just a nip. Then I'd get back to business.

Unable to help myself, I went over and knelt down by the body. Quaking with desire, I set the gun down, bent and touched my lips to the blood-slick neck. It wasn't until I heard the racking cough above me that I realized it had all been a trap. Of course it had. What vampire worth his salt would waste good blood spreading it around on the walls? He wouldn't, unless he was trying to lure another vampire to him by doing it.

Stupid.

Too late, I looked up to see Brasher, in full vampire form, upside down and clinging like a white spider to a light fixture on the high vaulted ceiling. Too late, I reached for the gun. Too goddamn late.

Brasher dropped down on me with an ugly snarl. His full weight caught me mid-back and slammed me down hard atop the dead kid. I grunted as one of my ribs broke with a garden-fresh snap. It hurt, don't think it didn't. For a moment I was pinned, helpless as a butterfly on a mat board, but then the pressure lifted and I lunged for the gun. My fingers fumbled for it, closed on it. Desperate, I rolled over to fire, but Brasher's clawed fist caught me on the jaw and drove me down on my back this time. Before I could react, his foot lashed out and kicked the gun from my hand, sending it clattering out of reach across the polished wood floor. Coraline was right; despite his age, he was unbelievably fast and strong. This was what it was to be a killing machine. I was in trouble and I knew it.

I tried to scramble back, but found myself stopped cold as a tree-root hand clamped down vice-tight on my windpipe. Brasher stuck his hideously malformed face—all bone and menace—in mine and lifted me until my patent leather shoe soles hovered a half-inch off the floor. It's a pretty good trick, unless you happen to be on the receiving end of it. He held me there, his blood-engorged eyes studying me like a lab specimen of considerable interest.

"So you're the one she's been slipping away to see," he said, his words sloppy and ill-formed as they fled through gaps in that awful mouth full of teeth. His breath smelled of blood and decay. "You don't look like much. I wonder what she sees in you."

"Guess you haven't seen your reflection lately," I managed through the choking.

It made him angry and he threw me across the room. I hit the far wall and bounced back like a pro-wrestler off the ropes, then collapsed in a heap on the floor.

Head spinning, ears ringing, my vision gray at the edges,

I curled up and waited for a final charge that didn't come. When I finally looked up, I saw Brasher in the final moments of transformation back into human form. As ugly a vampire as he made, he made an even uglier person. He looked like something dug up from a grave. Worse, he looked wrong, like a perversion of nature, far too old to still be walking and talking and sucking air.

"My apologies. I'm afraid I let my temper get the best of me," he wheezed. "Let's don't fight. At least until we ascertain precisely why we are fighting."

"Suits me," I said, glad for any reprieve in the beating.

Brasher started to say something else, but decided on a hacking fit of coughing instead. It wasn't pretty. With his looks, nothing he did would ever be pretty again. I averted my eyes, more for me than for him, and waited for it to end. When it finally did, he took a stained handkerchief from the pocket of his red-satin smoking jacket and dabbed it over his bloody lips.

"I think I may have overtaxed myself playing with you as I did," he said with a chuckle. Then, sucking for air like an old accordion, he stumbled over to one of the few chairs in the room that remained unbroken and upright and sank into it. "If you live to be my age you'll find that there's a hefty toll for everything you do."

I didn't know if he meant it in earnest or as a threat, but being as he had gone back to coughing, I decided to let it go.

This time, when he was done he said, "You came to kill me." It was a statement, not a question.

"How did you know?"

He nodded, smiled bitterly. "I've known for a while now. She tried her best to hide it, but, well I'm afraid it slipped out. Our little Coraline is quite a girl, isn't she?"

"Yeah," I agreed. "She's quite a girl." It seemed to say it all. Suddenly we were just two Joes in love with the same dame.

"I suppose I should have anticipated something like this. Of course it would end like this. Of course it would. I—it's just— she was so lovely I couldn't help myself." He looked at me as if to ask if I understood.

I nodded. I understood all too well.

"I suppose the saying 'There is no greater fool than an old fool' is true. It was stupid, but I allowed myself to believe she truly cared for me."

"Maybe that's what you get for turning a girl young enough to be your long-lost descendent."

Brasher nodded. "You're right, of course. I shouldn't have done it. I knew that, but I just wanted to experience the love of a woman one more time before—" He cut himself off with a shake of the head. "And then she was so insistent."

He must have seen something in my expression because he styled his mug into something resembling a smile. "That surprises you." A statement, not a question.

"You're saying she asked you to turn her into a vampire?"

"Demanded, to be precise. I don't know how she found out about me exactly, but there are a select few mortals who know what I am. It's unavoidable. In any case, she turned up here late one night. Waltzed right up to my front gate and told me over the speaker box that she had a proposition for me and wanted to be let in. I was intrigued. I let her in."

Brasher went through a pint-size version of the coughing and wiping routine before going on. I waited for him to finish before asking, "So what was it?"

"She told me I either had to make her into what I was, or else she was going straight to the police and make trouble for me with a story that I had tried to rape and kill her." He smiled like a proud poppa. "Can you imagine? Trying to blackmail me."

"What'd you do?"

"I told her there was one alternative she had overlooked. That if I wished I could simply kill her where she stood."

"And?"

"And that's when she showed me the gun. That very one right there I believe." He gestured behind me to where the pistol had come to a stop against a table leg. "She showed it to me and said she had a silver bullet for every step I took toward her. Brave little minx. Well, how could I resist a proposition like that?"

"So you turned her."

"I did."

"Funny, that's not the version I heard."

"Did you hear it, or did you see it?"

The expression on my face answered for me. Brasher nodded. "I thought so. You saw what she wanted you to see, nothing more."

"Nice try," I said.

"You think I'm prevaricating?"

"If that's a fancy way of saying I think you're full of horseshit, yeah, that's exactly what I think."

Brasher smiled. "Perhaps I'm not the biggest fool here. At least I know when I've been duped."

"That what you think? She duped me into this?"

"Of course. She needed you to kill me because she couldn't do it herself, so she convinced you that I'm a monster that needs to be put down. Simple as that."

"You're wrong."

Brasher only smiled at me.

"Why tell me all this? Why not just kill me?"

"My dear boy, why in the world would I do that? You're just a pawn in this game. Killing you would accomplish nothing, but turning you against your own queen, now that—that would be a feat."

"How do you plan to do that?"

"Simply by telling you the truth."

"Yeah? Okay, so what's the truth?"

"She's going to turn on you. She's already planning on it."

"Don't you say that. Don't you goddamn say that. You don't know a thing about me and her."

Brasher took a swipe at his lips and said, "Oh, but I do. When I realized she was slipping away to see someone else I couldn't resist. I took a peek into her mind. She plans on doing away with you too."

The pitying way he shook his head at me made me sore—real sore, if you want to know the truth. Forgetting myself, I reached out and grabbed him up by his lapels from the chair and shook him violently. "You're lying!"

"You wouldn't be so angry if you believed that."

"Take it back. Take it back or I'll kill you."

I slammed him hard against the wall, setting off a whole new fit of coughing. Thinking it would be impolite to interrupt, I just stood there waiting for him to die or recover. He recovered. When he did he said, "I accept."

"Come again?" I said, letting him go in my surprise.

Free, Brasher moved back to the chair and sat again. "I accept your proposition. You came to kill me and I'm going to let you."

"And why the hell would you do that?"

"You're too young to understand, but when you get to a certain point you know your time is done. Your best years are behind you; long behind in my case. Vampires live a long time, but even we don't live forever. That's what they don't tell you—that however slowly it happens, you continue to decay. I'm rotting. Falling apart from the inside out. Coraline was the only thing I've had worth living for in a month of years, and now I find I don't even have that. One final lesson well learnt. It's time."

Looking at him sitting there, slumped and broken, I knew he was right. He was a cautionary tale. He had lived far too long. I would be doing him a favor by killing him.

"How do you want it?" I asked.

"One has too few unexpected moments at my age," he said. "Why don't you surprise me."

The hazel-wood stake Coraline had given me remained jammed down in my belt. I took it out now and walked over to him and placed the tip against the satin cloth of his jacket, just over his heart.

"If I may give you one last avuncular word of advice," he said. "When you've done what you're going to do, I recommend that you drink some of my blood."

"Why would I do that?"

"For your own good. I made Coraline. She made you. With my blood in your veins she won't be able to look into your mind as I've done with her. The playing field will be level."

"Why are you so interested in helping me?"

"The way I see it, you and I are the victims here. When you realize I'm right about her, you'll kill her. But only if she doesn't see it coming and kill you first."

"You're wrong about her, old man," I said.

Brasher laughed patronizingly and I jammed the stake through his salmon-bone brittle breastplate and deep into his heart as much to cut the sound of it short as anything else. It must have hurt, but only a soft gasp escaped him as his jaundiced, seen-everything eyes grew wide and he folded like a collapsed tent to the floor.

Unblinking, those awful eyes watched me as I moved in and bit at his neck and drank. They watched me as I lifted him into my arms and carried him to the fireplace and folded him in like a marionette into its case. They watched me as I doused him with kerosene and scratched a match to life. Even as his clothes ignited and his flesh blackened and ran—

They watched me.

18

The pounding on the door signals the transition from one nightmare to another. I get up. I tell the pounder to hold his horses. I dress. When I finally answer I find two homicide detectives standing at my door. One I don't recognize. The other I do.

"Detective Coombs," I say, forcing a smile. Dumb luck. All the homicide detectives crawling around this city and I get Coombs twice in the same week.

"That's right. How'd you know?"

"Your message," I say, hoping there was one.

"Oh right. Right. You uh—" He checks his notes. "You Michael Angel?"

I nod and give him my firmest good-guy handshake.

"Hey, wow. Your hands are cold."

"Bad circulation," I say, not bothering to mention it's because I've spent the last twelve hours in a deep freeze.

Coombs nods and a look of puzzlement crosses his doughy

face. "Have we met?"

"Oh I think I'd remember that," I say.

Coombs doing what he does and me doing what I do, I guess it's only natural we'd bump into each other from time to time, but the fact that this visit follows so closely on the heels of our last makes me uneasy. Real uneasy, if you want to know the truth.

"Hey, where are my manners? This is my partner, Detective Elliot," Coombs says.

I shake Elliot's hand and study him while he does the same to me. He's younger and thinner than Coombs with a snarl of curly brown hair that could still be weeded of its gray. What his face lacks in chin it tries to make up for in nose. The overall effect makes his head look top-heavy. Taken together they couldn't be more different. The only things they have in common are the cheap suits and the bacon-smelling aftershave.

"Mind if we come in?"

"Actually, I'm kind of in a hurry. I have an appointment."

"It won't take long," Elliot says, speaking for the first time. His voice is nasal and a little whiny and I imagine it's the reason he leaves most of the talking to Coombs.

It all sounds polite and friendly, but I can tell I don't really have a choice here, so I let them in. I figure this visit has to do with either Dallas or Vin Prince. Problem is I don't know which and it doesn't seem like a good idea to ask.

Coombs and I sit at my desk just like before. I apologize to Elliot for not having an extra chair.

"That's all right. I like to stand. Like to move around,"

he says. As if to prove the point he walks over and picks the photograph of me and my old band mates up off my desk and looks at it.

"This you?"

I shake my head. "My grandpa."

"Looks just like you."

"That's what Grandma always said," I say with a thin smile. "So, uh, what's all this about?"

"You in a hurry?" Coombs asks now.

"I think I said I was."

"Oh that's right, you did say that. You're going somewhere, right?"

"Yeah," I say, as Elliot circles behind me like a shark to inspect the aluminum foil covered window.

"Big date?"

"Something like that," I say.

"What's the deal with this?" Elliot asks now, aiming one narrow finger at my window. This must be how they do it. Keep the questions coming hard and fast and keep the suspect off balance. Got to give it to them—it worked.

"It gets hot in here during the day with that eastern exposure. The foil helps keep it cooler."

"Gotcha." Seemingly satisfied, Elliot nods and moves on.

I turn my attention back to Coombs. "So, why are you fellas here?"

"Oh, well, see, uh, turns out your name came up in a little investigation we're working on."

"That right?" I ask.

He nods, scratches his nose. "Mmm-hmm."

"What kind of investigation?"

"Homicide. Your name turned up in the phone logs of the decedent."

It's my turn to nod. In my peripheral vision, I see Detective Elliot pluck at the fabric over the knees of his suit pants and stoop down and pull the door of my mini-fridge open.

"Would you mind not doing that?" I say. You have to draw the line with cops or else they take compliance as a sign of guilt.

"Why not? You don't have anything to hide, do ya?" Elliot says with a smile.

I see his smile and raise him a grin. "Sure. Doesn't everybody?"

He laughs and looks inside anyway. It's empty. Before turning in last night I made a point of stashing what remained of Vin's blood in a cooler in an unmarked grave I keep in a certain well-known city park just in case I ever need to go to ground for a while. I also stashed my kit, my satchel, my gun, and some of Leroy's cash there. Right now I feel very glad I did.

I turn back to Coombs, who consults a notepad he has taken out. "Are you familiar with a woman by the name of Callie-Dean Merriweather?"

I plaster a puzzled look to my mug and slowly shake my head back and forth. "I don't think s—"

"She's a stripper and part-time call girl. Goes by the stage name Dallas."

"Oh, Dallas," I say, nodding now. "I know Dallas."

"How well?"

"Not very."

Coombs nods. "You happen to remember the last time you saw her?"

This is where a stupid person would lie. I'm no genius but I know enough to spot a trap when I see one. Cops rarely ask a question they don't already know the answer to. Not if they're any good they don't.

"Sure. Just the other night. I went into the club where she works to see her."

Coombs nods, scribbles notes. "What for?"

"Her name came up in a case I'm working on."

"That's right, you're a detective yourself, aren'tcha?" He says it with the patronizing tone all cops use with all private detectives. It makes me sore, but I let it go with a nod.

"What's the case?"

"Missing person. I'm helping a girl find her fourteen year-old sister who's run away."

"And you thought this Dallas might know something?"

"That's right. I heard through the grapevine that she knew the girl."

"So you went to ask her about it."

"That's right," I say again.

At this point Elliot jumps in to let me know he's parched and to inquire after a glass of water.

"Sure," I say. I start to get up, but he waves me back down.

"Don't trouble yourself. I'll get it." He points at the doorway that leads to my little kitchenette. "Through there?"

I nod. He exits. I turn back to Coombs.

"So you went and talked to Dallas about this missing girl."

"Right."

"And was she helpful?"

"Not very."

"I gotcha. So then you left?"

"Right."

"And that's the last time you saw her?"

He's good. Real good. I see the potential to walk smack into another trap, but this time I'm not sure how to field it. I don't know how much he knows. If I admit to going to Dallas's house later, then I've just put myself at the scene of the crime on the night she was killed, but if I lie and Coombs knows I was there then I become his number one suspect.

I'm saved from answering by Elliot's appearance in the doorway. He has a mug of water in one hand and a perplexed look on his face.

"You know you have a buncha dirt in your freezer?"

"Yeah," I say. "What were you doing in my freezer?"

"Looking for ice cubes," he says. "Mind if I ask why you keep dirt in there?"

"I like my dirt cold," I tell him, and turn back to Coombs who's looking at me like he's still waiting for an answer. "Sorry. What was the question?"

"I asked if the club was the last place you saw Dallas."

I stall by fumbling for my pack and lighting a cigarette. The more I think about it, the more I see I've been looking at this all wrong. I've been trying to minimize the amount of trouble I'm in, when I should be thinking about the greatest possible gain. On the one hand, if I tell them I was there and they don't know it, I put myself at the top of their death penalty 'to do' list. On the other hand, if I lie and they do know it, all I'll be doing is confirming what they already know. It won't look good, but I'm already in deep and a little deeper won't make much difference. Either way, if I'm there I'm screwed. It's just a matter of degrees. I don't exactly have the kind of lifestyle that can bear a lot of scrutiny—or any for that matter. The only way I can hope to come out ahead is if I walk away from this interrogation farther off their radar than I was to start with, and the only way to do that is to lie and hope these coppers are dumber than I think. So I lie.

"Right. Yeah, that's the last place I saw her," I say.

I can tell from the look that passes between the detectives it's the wrong answer. I can smell their high-octane excitement as adrenaline dumps into their bloodstreams and pumps from their pores. They have me. I don't know why or how, but they have me.

"Would you mind coming downtown with us, Mr. Angel?" Coombs says.

"What for?"

Coombs shrugs. "Just to talk."

Elliot nods confirmation.

"We're talking now."

"We'd prefer to continue downtown," Elliot says. "That way we can get your statement. Make it official."

This time Coombs nods agreement.

"Well I'd like to, but I can't. Like I said, I have an

appointment."

"I think you're going to have to reschedule it," Coombs says.

"We're going to have to insist," Elliot says.

I notice that he has moved between me and the door while we've been talking.

"Could you guys at least tell me what this is about?"

"Sure. We'll explain everything. Downtown," Coombs says.

"Downtown," Elliot nods.

I sit, watching my cigarette burn to ash like a vampire at dawn, and consider my options. There aren't many. As I see it I can either take a ride downtown like they want, or rough them up and disappear, or kill them both. I can't say I like any of them much. I don't like cops as a rule—never have—but these two haven't done anything to make me think they might deserve killing. My gut tells me they're on the up-and-up, and thirsty as I am, I have rules about that sort of thing. Roughing them up and disappearing is probably the safest route to go, but vampires are creatures of habit. You get used to a place over time. You get comfortable. Call it a fatal flaw. Except for the time I spent up in San Quentin, I've lived in Los Angeles my whole life long. It's home. I don't want to go through the trouble of finding a new place. A new life. I will if I have to—we all do what we have to—but I'd need to know just exactly how bad my situation is to commit to a course of action that drastic.

One last drag and I stand with a smokescreen sigh. "All right," I say. "Let's go downtown."

Turns out it's bad—real bad—and they enjoy telling me all

about it in the claustrophobic little closet of an interrogation room they stick me in when we get where we're going. They tell me about how one of the other strippers remembered Dallas dancing for several Midwestern insurance salesmen in town for a convention. And about how she left with one of them at the end of the night. And about how they managed to catch up with him at his Burbank hotel room just hours before he caught a flight out of town. And about how the guy had a busted nose when they found him. And about how it got that way because of a certain S.O.B.—his words not theirs—who was waiting in the house for Dallas when they arrived back that night. And about the description he gave them of the S.O.B.

"Imagine our surprise when we show up at your place and you fit the description," Elliot says, enjoying himself. "Funny huh?"

"Hilarious," I say.

"Well if you like that, you'll really get a kick outa this," Coombs tells me.

"The insurance salesman is on his way over here as we speak to take a look at the lineup we've arranged. Should be here any time now."

Coombs and Elliot share a look of great amusement.

"You okay, pal?" Coombs asks.

"I'm fine," I say, faking a smile. It's a lie and he knows it.

It's funny, all the people I've killed over the years and the only two times I've ever been in any kind of real trouble for murder it's been over ones I didn't commit. If I wasn't so capital-letter-f-Fucked I'd probably bust a gut over it.

Coombs assumes my sickly reaction is due to all the bad

news he just unloaded on me, but he's only half right. The fact is my need is growing. I haven't had a fix since shooting my fill of Vin's blood last night. It has held me over this long, but now my junkie hands are getting shifty on me and I'm starting to perspire. Just a little right now, but it will get worse. A lot worse. Already my fingers have taken on the translucent bleached-white color that comes with blood starvation. In vampires, the need for blood starts in the extremities and works its way in toward the heart; much like crucifixion. As the need grows, a cramping, Charlie horse-like pain gradually invades your limbs, your torso, your chest, until, racked with agony, all you can do is lay like a curled dead spider on the floor and pray for relief from an uncaring God.

Obviously I'm going to have to do something before my old pal Tom arrives and seals my fate, but I'd like to do it the non-bloody legal way.

If I can.

"We know you were there, Mick," Coombs says, seated across the burn-scarred table top from me. The sister smells of desperation and fear emanate from it in waves; ghost emotions cast off by all those who have squirmed here before me. "Why don't you just make it easy on yourself and come clean?"

"Yeah," Elliot says, slouching cross-armed under the camera rigged in one corner of the room. "I mean, just because you were there doesn't mean you did it. But if you keep lying about it, what do you expect us to think?"

"We want to help you, Mick," Coombs says. "Help us help you."

I groan inwardly. The only thing worse than good cop, bad cop is good cop, good cop.

"All right," I say. "I'll talk. But I want my phone call first."

Coombs smiles like he wants to be my buddy, but I'm making it difficult. "Why don't we hold off on that for a little bit?" he says.

"How 'bout a soda instead?" Elliot says.

They finally give me my call when they know there's no chance I can get a lawyer down here before the lineup. A blue-suited uni takes me to a greasy pay phone in a hallway as sallow and dead-end as I feel and leaves me to it. Because of the lack of blood in them, my fingers are even more numb and useless than usual and it takes all my concentration just to get them to punch up Reesa's cell phone number. She answers. I've caught her between shows. It's the first bit of good luck I've had all night.

"Hi, doll," I say.

"Mick, where have you been? I've been trying to call you." The sound of genuine concern in her voice reminds me just how long it's been since I had anyone who gave a shit about me. It's nice. Real nice, if you want to know the truth.

"Ran into a little trouble on the case. One of the girls I questioned ended up dead."

"Who?"

"A stripper by the name of Dallas your sister stayed with for a little while before taking off again."

"And the police think you had something to do with it?"

"I think that's safe to say."

"Oh my God. That's awful."

"It's not good," I agree.

"Why do they think you were involved?"

"No reason, except they think they can put me at the scene."

"That's it? What about a motive?"

"They don't care about that. The prosecutor can always make one up later."

"But you didn't even know Callie. Why would you want to kill her?"

"I wouldn't, but you can't talk to cops. They have a guy they think can put me at the scene and they've arranged a lineup for him to do it."

"Who?"

"Some insurance salesman—Tom something. He says some guy busted his nose at Dallas's place the night she died and he's on his way over here now to see if it was me. I was hoping maybe you knew a lawyer—a good one—who might be able to get down here quick and help me out."

"Of course. I'll make a call," she says.

"I'd appreciate it."

She tells me to be careful. She tells me to come see her when I get out. I tell her I will and get off.

Maybe it's because I'm feeling so blood-sick, or maybe it's because I have so damn much on my mind, but it isn't until the flatfoot puts me back in my pen that I realize I never told her Dallas's real name.

Handcuffed to the table, I sit and wait.

Time passes like a ticking bomb.

I can only assume I've been set up, but I can't figure out why. I try to think it through, but I don't get anywhere. The need has become so bad it's impossible for me to think straight. The cramping has worked its way past the joints in my arms and legs. My aching head feels like it's been packed full with gauze. My brain cells are too starved of blood to do anything but drone out a steady busy signal. I only know two things. One, I've been betrayed by a woman I care about. Again. And two, I need to get the hell out of here but fast.

I shouldn't have come in the first place. I should have known better. Dumb. But there's nothing for it now. I decide to wait for my best opportunity. Probably after the lineup when they take me for booking and processing. Then I'll snap the cuffs and take one of the detectives hostage before they know what's hit them. I'll drag him along using him as a shield as I fight my way out past bars and guns and guards. With a little luck I won't take a bullet in the head or the spine. It doesn't seem too much to ask. Problem with that is, the odds are always with the house.

Knowing I'm being watched on camera, I rest my throbbing head on the table and try not to think about blood or betrayal.

I wind up thinking about both.

1946

With Brasher out of the way, Coraline and I took up residence in that big old drafty house of his. She had already figured out how to get her hands on the money in his various bank accounts. So we moved on in, and spent his money and lived as if we didn't have a care in the world. As if there never was a Brasher and he had never told me that the woman I loved was going to betray me.

I couldn't forget his warning, but as time passed I found I could dismiss it. Because he was wrong. Coraline and I loved each other. Lots had changed. Almost everything. But not that. Never that. Some things you just have to take on faith.

While we were planning the murder Coraline had done all the hunting for us so as not to distract me from the task at hand. After we moved into the house though, she decided it was time I learned to hunt for myself. At first, I put her off. The whole idea of hunting people sickened me. I wanted no part in it. But she kept at me about it. She viewed my reluctance as a weakness. We fought.

"You're being silly. You're not human, you're something greater now. A vampire. There aren't any rules for us any more," she said.

"Maybe there should be."

"Don't be silly. We're the top of the food chain. Humans are just take-out food to us."

"Well maybe I don't like what's on the menu."

Coraline sneered now. She had always been a good sneerer and death hadn't changed that any. "Don't be a hypocrite. You like it. You like it just swell when I do the hunting and all you have to do is feed, when you don't have to think about where the blood came from."

I realized she was right. I was a hypocrite. I did like it. A lot. And after all, just because you let the butcher slaughter the pig for you doesn't mean you don't have a hand in its death.

She wanted me to go on a hunt with her and in the end I went. We drove to the outskirts of the city where small developments of cheap tract houses were being bought up by G.I.s returning home from the war.

We ended up at a modest two-story with a wide front porch in an unfinished cul-de-sac. Other houses on the block were being built, but so far this was the only one finished. Coraline thought it was just right.

The lights were on in the family room and we watched in silence through a large front porch window as a young man, tie undone and legs up on the coffee table, and his pretty wife cozied up on a couch and looked at the T.V. together.

Seeing them, seeing how safe and content they seemed, how in love and happy, I wanted to go somewhere else and told Coraline so, but she refused.

"No. We're going in here," she said.

"Coraline, I'll do this, okay? I'll hunt, but not here. Not them."

"You're weak, Mick, you know that?" she said, her eyes ugly and derisive. "It's embarrassing."

I tried to grab and hold her, but she broke away and marched to the door and rang the bell. When the man answered, she pretended her car had broken down just up the road and asked if she could use a phone to call for help. He invited her in. Folks were more trusting in those days. Knowing I was out there watching, Coraline smiled at me out the window as he lead her into the family room to introduce her to his wife.

A sick, tight feeling in my stomach, I watched her break the man's neck. Turning, Coraline looked at the wife still trying to make sense of it all on the couch and allowed her fangs to distend. I listened to the wife's pitiful scream as she stood and for the first time I saw she was pregnant. Filled with horror, the woman ran for the stairs, arms cradled around her bulging belly. Frozen in place, stunned by the awful spectacle unfolding on the other side of the thin pane of glass, I watched Coraline smile hungrily as she transformed and gave chase.

I moved then. I ran to the door, flung it open, and raced up the stairs and down a long hall toward the master bedroom where I could hear sounds of a struggle. It was too late by the time I got there. Too goddamn late. The woman was already dead, her neck snapped backward. If that had been the worst of it, it would have been bad enough, but it wasn't. On the floor by the four-post bed, her face covered in gore, Coraline sat feeding on the unborn child she had ripped from the dead woman's belly.

She looked up when she sensed me standing in the doorway, strings of blood hanging from her fangs. She smiled and held the child out to me.

"Hungry, baby?"

For the first time I saw behind the mask. Really saw. Sure, I'd caught glimpses in the past—like when she murdered Roy—but I had always been able to explain it away. I told myself with all she had been through growing up she had good reason to do what she'd done to him, at least in her own mind. Now I realized she was a broken thing and always had been and I had just seen what she showed me; what she wanted me to see. Hard as it was to accept, I suddenly realized the girl I loved didn't really exist and never had. She was just smoke and lies and mirrors.

Coraline's laughter chased me back the way I'd come; up the hall and down the stairs. I made it as far as the porch railing before throwing up in the landscaped bushes that ran along the front of the house. The same bushes no one would come out in the morning on their way to work and decide needed a trim.

Hunched there, smelling the sour fumes of my own sick, I realized that Coraline was wrong. There had to be rules. Even for vampires. Rules gave meaning to an otherwise mindless existence. Without them, thinking beings were reduced to feeding, fighting, and fucking just because it was in their nature. If there was any point to any of this, then there had to be an attempt to rise above one's nature; to be better than one's basest needs and desires. Otherwise we were no better than animals.

None of us.

As it turned out, that night was a test. One we both failed. In my eyes Coraline was a monster and in hers I was weak and unworthy.

I knew for sure that everything had changed when I awakened two nights later to find Coraline looming silently over my opened coffin.

"What are you doing, Coraline?" I asked her, trying to keep the cold terror that was creeping into my guts out of my voice.

"Just watching you sleep, baby," she said with an emotionless smile that didn't reach her eyes. "You know how I've always liked to watch you sleep."

After she had disappeared in darkness and gone to hunt, I lay there thinking for a long time. Brasher had been right. Whether or not she had planned to before, I knew now that the woman I loved intended to kill me and the only way I could stop her was by killing her first.

Problems just don't get much worse than that.

I felt like Brasher; old and disappointed and too worn out to care. I'd given up everything for the love of a woman and found it was nothing more substantial than a morning mist that burns away with the first light of day. She was the reason I'd done it all; the reason I'd become this thing I hated.

I considered taking my own life then. Just ending it. I had

died for her before, I could do it again. One final gift. It would have been the easy way out, but if I did it I knew that Coraline would only go on committing atrocities. If I went that route— if I didn't do anything to stop her—every innocent life she took from that point on would be on my shoulders. I couldn't have that. Whether it was a murder or a murder/suicide, she had to go. After that I could decide if I wanted to live on without her or not, but on that one point I was clear. Coraline needed to be put down.

My mind made up, I went and waited for the woman I loved to come home so I could kill her.

Of course, in the end it wasn't as simple as that.

Things with Coraline never were.

CORALINE

Things with Coraline ended like they started. With a bullet. I was waiting in the darkened study when she returned from her hunt. Coraline was as surprised to see me sitting there alone in the dark as I was to see the child in her arms. A lovely blonde-haired girl of about six in a black crushed velvet dress and shiny black metal-buckled shoes.

"Look what I found," she said merrily, holding the petrified child up for me to see. It made me feel sick to see the building terror in those sweet young eyes. "Doesn't she look positively scrumptious, Mick?"

"Put her down," I said.

"I will. Just as soon as I have a little taste."

"You're not going to hurt that child."

Coraline laughed her windchime laugh as if she found me both ridiculous and amusing. She always did like to laugh at me. When she sobered she smiled circumspectly. "Now Mick, let's don't fight. You don't have to join in, but don't go telling me my business. I do what I want. You know that."

"Put her down," I said again, showing her the .38 now. Coraline stared at it. For a moment I thought I saw fear flicker in her eyes. Her fingers tightened slightly, leaving imprints on the little girl's soft pink flesh.

"If I didn't know better I'd think you were threatening me."

"I am."

"That's a mistake, lover."

"Well, we all make 'em," I said. "Just like you made one when you sent me to kill Brasher."

"How was that a mistake?"

"Because he told me things."

"Like what?"

"Like how you used me," I said. "You needed me to kill him because you couldn't do it yourself and turned me into a monster to do it."

"No. I saved you. They were going to execute you."

"They did execute me, baby," I said. "But if you'd really wanted you could've gotten me outa there before they did it. You could have gotten me off the row any number of ways, but you didn't. You traded on my feelings for you and you turned me."

"Is that what this is about?"

I smiled bitterly. "It's about a lot of things."

"So what now, lover? You gonna kill me?"

I looked at her, taking in those glamour-girl features I used to like so much before I glimpsed what lurked behind them, and shrugged. "I guess maybe I am."

Coraline shook her head at me. "You can't do it."

"You sure about that?"

She nodded. "You can't do it because you and I—we were made for each other, baby."

I snorted. "Yeah we've got something real special."

"What do you want? You want me to stop feeding on women and children. I'll do it. I'll do whatever you want."

Coraline bent and set the terrified child gently on the floor at her feet. "There, you see?"

"Too late for that," I said.

"It's not. It can't be," she said, moving like the shadow of death across the floor to me.

"Stay back, Coraline."

"No. I won't. It can't end this way. I won't let it. Not after all we've meant to each other. I may have made mistakes, Mick—I know I have—but I always loved you."

"Too late for that too."

"Stop saying that. It's not too late. I could have killed you in your sleep earlier and I didn't. I didn't because we've stepped through a door together. We're on the yellow brick road and there's no going back. Not ever. We need each other. That's what I realized."

She was right about one thing. This was Oz and I was the idiot Scarecrow and the sleeve-hearted Tin Man and the yellowbelly Lion all rolled into one. Even knowing all I knew, my heart was telling me one thing and my brain another and I was too damn scared to pick between them. Pathetic.

"Fine." A defiant look in her eye, Coraline took hold of

the barrel of the gun and placed it dead center between her breasts. "If you can look me in the eye and tell me you don't love me then shoot me, Mick. Kill me. I want you to. None of this is worth a damn thing to me if you don't."

My head spun like a Kansas twister as I focused on the gun, trying to get right about what I needed to do. It was so clear before, but now it was no good. I was just as under her spell as I had always been.

"You have to change," I said. "You have to."

"I will, baby. I will. You'll see."

"It can't be like this. We have to have rules."

"We will. Whatever you want. Whatever you say."

"Promise me."

She looked me earnestly. "I promise."

Shaking with emotion, I dropped my arm to my side and let the gun clatter to the floor.

Coraline wrapped her arms around me like twin white snakes and pulled me close. "There now, you see—it's all going to be okay, darling. So long as we have each other," she said, pressing her cool wet mouth to mine.

She tasted like fate.

When it came, the bullet took me by surprise; she always was good at surprising me. Looking down I saw the big ugly gaping red mouth the double-barrel Derringer she held had torn in my gut. Coraline smiled at me. Eyes on that smile, I stumbled back as the pain set in, fierce as a chemical burn. It was bad. Real bad, if you want to know the truth. But it didn't hurt me half as much as that smile, because some smiles just hurt worse than bullets.

"Silver bullets?" I asked, jaw clenched against the pain.

"Only the best for you," she said. "I got the gun special while I was out tonight. I was going to seduce you and then kill you while you slept in my arms—send you off with a bang—but this will work too." She thumbed the hammer back on the second barrel and took aim. "Sorry, baby."

The second bullet caught me in the neck. It was probably intended for my head, but I had benefited from the Derringer's well-documented lack of accuracy. It was meant for close work. A whore's gun. Seemed appropriate.

I collapsed on my back to the floor.

Dropping the empty pistol, Coraline moved toward me, fangs distending and eyes blackening as she came. Weak from blood loss and pain, I could only watch as she settled down atop me as she had so many times before. Only it wasn't love she was after this time, it was death. Her fangs bit deep into my neck wound and I felt my life's blood sucked from me in a torrent. The world grayed at the edges and I knew it was too late. This was how it would end.

Then something brushed my fingertips. Moving only my eyes, I saw the child over Coraline's shoulder crouched nearby. Wide-eyed and silent, she had slipped up and pushed the .38 into reach. I can't imagine the resolve it must have taken, the sheer terror she must have overcome to do it, but I didn't have time to think about it. My heart was already beginning to sputter like an engine low on fuel.

I grabbed the gun, shoved it between us and emptied it into

my dark angel. Gravely hurt, Coraline sagged atop me.

We lay there on the floor like spent lovers, and then, little by little, I inched myself within reach of her neck. I admired the cool Elizabethan white of it, kissed her to mark the spot, and then I let my fangs distend and I fed.

I drank her to the cliff's edge of death, then I stopped and looked into her eyes. Without blood to sustain her, her skin was paper white. She looked withered; atrophied like some of the terminally ill I had seen during my time in the hospital. I could sense her pain. And her seething hatred. But mostly I could sense her fear. Her fear of the ever after and the punishment she suddenly worried might await her there.

As I watched, she turned back. Her eyes drained of blood. Her fangs and brow receded. Her jaw re-hinged. And for a moment I saw the girl I had met at that club way back when. The one I'd taken a fall for I could never get up from. My precious doe-eyed beauty who wanted to see the dark side of the world at any cost, and who had recognized in me the sucker who could show it to her. Well, she'd gotten her wish, hadn't she?

Sure she had.

I pushed Coraline off me and somehow managed to get to my feet. The study door was open and the girl was gone. Off hiding somewhere. Smart kid.

With great effort I bent and picked Coraline up and carried her to the cold stone fireplace where I had burnt Brasher. Curled like the baby Jesus in a manger of ashes, her eyes followed me as I moved off and returned bearing a tin of kerosene.

I stood over her, trying to come up with something more to say, but there wasn't anything. It had all been said and none of it had made a bit of difference. It was over. Everything was over. I hunted up a cigarette to fill the silence instead.

Coraline shuddered slightly as I doused her with the kerosene. It matted her hair and ran down her face and stung her eyes. She looked at me forlornly as I struck a long wooden fireplace match and lit my smoke with it. Her lips moved in a silent plea.

"Sorry, baby," I said.

The match seemed to take a lifetime to fall. The first flames licked at her uncertainly, as if sampling an unfamiliar dish for the first time, and then deciding they liked the taste, rose and consumed her. Heartbroken and full of regret, I watched her blacken and die a vampire's death. Like Brasher before her, Coraline's eyes never left mine. Near the end, her lovely lips twitched again, but her final words to me were lost in a sigh of death and release.

Knowing I could never live here now, I spilled more kerosene and set the whole place ablaze. If I hadn't had the kid to worry about I might just have sat down and let myself burn up with it. But I did. With Coraline's death I'd sealed a pact to rise above my nature. To be better.

I found her hiding among dust bunnies under a canopied bed in a darkened guestroom. She let out a piercing brain-freeze scream and kicked her buckled shoes at me as I bent and peered at her under the dust ruffle.

"It's okay," I said. "It's me."

She didn't respond, so I asked her name.

"'Lizabeth."

"That's a pretty name. Okay, Elizabeth, c'mon, let's get you home."

She trembled like a rabbit as I helped her out from underneath and lifted her small form into my arms. She grabbed onto my neck for dear life and I carried her from the house like that as it burned down around us. Outside, the growing wail of sirens pierced the night like screams of horror. I loaded her into the passenger seat of Brasher's Cadillac, went around, got in.

"I want my mommy," she whispered, as I started the car up and put it in gear.

"Me too, kid," I said.

She just looked at me. I just drove.

21

Through the red haze of pain racking my body I come around to find Coombs and Elliot in the interrogation room with me again. I'm so out of it I've totally missed their entrance.

"What's going on? You on the drugs, son?" Coombs asks.

"Son" he calls me. I'm old enough to have banged his grandmother. Hell, maybe I did.

"Looks like narcotic withdrawal to me," Elliot says.

If he only knew. What I'm going through at present makes narcotic withdrawal look like a day at the beach. I would know.

"You play ball with us, maybe we could get you a little something to help you out with that. Something to take the edge off," Coombs says.

The only thing that's going to take the edge off at this point is running through his fat-clogged arteries. The way things are looking, I might just have to take him up on that offer. I'm going to have to get some blood in me if I'm going to get out of here. I'm in too much pain, too weakened to escape without it.

The door opens and the blue-suit who took me to make my phone call steps in.

"The witness here?" Coombs asks.

The blue-suit nods. "We're all set up."

"Good."

"Sure you don't want to make a confession before we go through with this, Angel?" Elliot asks me. "It'll be too late to cooperate after this guy fingers you."

"Okay, I confess—I think your nose is way too big for your face. Makes you look like one of those caricatures they draw down at Venice Beach." I smile. The pain is making me mean.

The punch comes from Coombs. A hard one in the gut. It knocks the breath out of me, doubles me over the table.

"You didn't see that," Coombs says to the uni still standing in the doorway.

"See what?" the guy says, an ugly grin spread over the lower half of his face like bacon grease.

"You know, you're a pretty funny guy, Angel," Elliot says, leaning close. "But guess who's gonna be laughin' when you're sitting on your ass on death row?"

"Been there, done that."

"Fuckin' guy's delusional," Elliot says.

"Whaddya expect? He's a junkie," Coombs says with disgust. "C'mon, let's get this over with before he starts shittin' an' pukin' himself."

They uncuff me and drag me off to the lineup.

It's me and seven other guys, most of them grungy looking

undercover cops. We stand in front of a one-way mirror under bright lights and a series of numbers. We go through the usual process. Me, I'm lucky number seven.

An authoritative voice comes over the loudspeaker. "Number six step forward."

Six, a denim-clad beanpole with a scraggly beard and greasy ponytail, steps forward.

"Say the line," the voice says.

"That's as good as it's going to get around here for you," six says, just like the five others before him did.

"Step back."

Six steps back.

"Seven, step forward."

I feel like I'm going to collapse any minute, but until then I do as I'm told.

"Say the line."

I say it.

"Step back."

I step back and wait while number eight goes through the rigmarole. Then I wait some more. I sense the eyes on me from the other side. They don't know it, but if I strain I can hear them talking. Faintly.

Coombs asks Tom if any of us look familiar to him and I am surprised to hear Tom say, "No."

"Take another look, Mr. Kelley," Elliot says, a note of irritation in his voice. "Take your time."

I feel the eyes on me again.

"No. None of them," Tom says at last.

Elliot says something in irritation that I miss, then Coombs pipes up. "You gave us a description of the guy you saw that night. Read it to him, Ray."

Paper rustles and Elliot reads from something. "Caucasian. About six foot. A hundred seventy pounds. Dark hair and eyes. Pale. Unshaven."

"Your words," Coombs says. "You telling me you don't see anyone in there that meets that description?"

"Yeah, sure," Tom says. "But I don't see anyone I recognize."

"How 'bout you take a guess," Elliot says. "Pretend you have to give us someone so we don't start thinking you were the last person to see the girl alive."

"Is that a threat?" Tom asks.

"No, sir. But look at it from our perspective. You say there was someone else there that night. We only have your word for it. If you can't give us something more to go on than that, then we have to at least consider the possibility that maybe there wasn't, don't we?"

"You do whatever you have to, Detective, but I'm not going to pin a murder on someone I don't think did it just 'cause they fit a description. That would be wrong."

"Wrong. You mean like a married father of three taking a stripper home from a club at three in the morning?" Coombs asks.

Tom's voice gets tight. "You're right. I shouldn'ta been there, but I didn't have anything to do with that girl's death. If you think I did then arrest me. Otherwise I'm catching a red-eye home to Des Moines tonight."

There's a tension-filled pause, then Coombs says, "Get him outa here."

I hear the sounds of shuffling, a door open and close, and Elliot say, "You think he did it?"

"That guy couldn't kill a fly," Coombs says. "Besides, someone was there that night. Someone busted his nose."

"Maybe it was the girl. Maybe that's why she's dead."

"There wasn't any sign of a struggle. She didn't have any of his blood on her. No, I think the son-of-a-bitch that did it is standing right in there."

There's a long pause and I feel their eyes on me.

"Whaddya wanna do with him?"

"Look at him. He's at breaking point. Let him sweat a little longer. Then we'll take one more stab at getting a confession out of him."

I sweat bullets waiting for them to come back. When they finally do, they come in and stand over me and stare, trying to build the suspense. Too bad for them I've already seen the end of this picture.

Finally, Elliot looks at Coombs and says, "You wanna tell him or should I?"

"I told the last guy. You do the honors," Coombs says.

Elliot looks at me and shrugs matter-of-factly. "The guy fingered ya, Angel. Picked you out first try."

Even if I hadn't heard all that had gone on, I'd have been able to sniff this whopper out.

"Tell you what, though. You come clean with us right now,

sign a full confession, and we'll tell the D.A. you gave it to us before the lineup. Make it look like you were cooperating all along."

"It'll go a lot better for you that way," Coombs says. "Might even be able to get a plea."

Even with all the pain I'm in I can't help but smile at the ploy. Lying is all part of the game. Cops lie during interrogations all the time. There's no law that says they can't. It's funny. They lie, they're pursuing justice. You lie, you're obstructing it.

"Hey, pal," Coombs says, "you just got picked as the main suspect in a capital murder case. You'll be lucky you don't get the needle for this. You think there's something funny in that?"

"Yeah I think it's funny," I tell him. "I think it's funny you two think this bullshit lie is gonna get you a confession."

"You think we're lying to you?" Elliot says all shocked and offended-like.

"I know you are. That guy couldn't have picked me out of the lineup."

"Oh? And why not?" Coombs asks.

"Because I was never in that goddamn house."

22

I'm on the street again a half hour later. I'm weak as hell and in a world of hurt, but at least I'm free.

To fix.

I make sure I'm not being tailed, then I hail a cab to Griffith Park. I sense the driver thinks it's more than a little strange to be dropping someone off here at this hour. I could explain it's because I need to find a grave where I stashed the human blood I need to survive, but I don't think it will ease his apprehensions any. I pay him instead and disappear into shadow.

I find the grave and dig with hands like garden trowels. I locate my kit and the cooler of dry ice and vials of blood. I'm so blood-deprived I can hardly feel my hands at all anymore and it's a world-class struggle just to tie my arm off and get the blood in the needle. It's even more difficult to find a vein and depress the plunger. Somehow I manage. I am a pro after all.

I shoot all the blood I have left. It's not enough. Not near enough after the starvation I've just gone through, but it will have to do. I've got a busy night ahead of me.

Places to go. People to bleed.

I need information and there's only one person I know of who can give it to me. Problem is he's blowing town.

I call the airports looking for red-eyes to Des Moines from a grungy Hollywood pay phone. I find two. Both out of LAX. Both leaving in less than an hour.

There's no time to go and get my car so I whistle up another cab. I tell him to take me to the airport and step on it.

From across the terminal I watch Tom wait for his plane. It's not much of a show. When he gets up for a last-minute bathroom break, I follow. I follow him into the bathroom and past the sinks and right into a stall. I'm standing there when he turns around to shut the door.

"What the—?"

I clamp a hand down hard over his mouth and force him down onto the toilet seat.

"I'm gonna do the asking, Tom, and if you don't want to get hurt, you're gonna do the answering and that's all you're gonna do. Understand?"

He nods. He understands. He's scared, which bothers me not at all. In my experience people tend to give better answers quicker that way.

I shut the door for privacy and squat so we're eye to eye. "You know who I am?"

He nods, his taped-up nose bobbing up and down. "You were one of the guys from the lineup."

I nod back. "Okay, so what gives? Who put you up to it?"

"Huh?"

"The lie you told the cops. Who put you up to it?"

"What are you talkin' about? I didn't lie to the cops."

"Cut the horseshit. You saw me. You saw me at the stripper's house that night, just like they said. I broke your nose. I made you leave."

"You're crazy, guy. You're fuckin' crazy. Before that lineup I'd never seen you before in my whole life."

I stare at Tom. The crazy thing—the really shithouse nuts thing—is he believes it. My stomach knots up on me the way it does at times like this; bad times when things turn out to be a whole hell of a lot worse than I thought and aren't likely to get any better.

I look him in the eye. "You never saw me. We never talked."

"Never talked," Tom mumbles agreeably.

"You catch that flight home and don't come back."

"Don't come back," he says.

I exit, leaving him seated pants-up on the john.

23

I grab an airport taxi home. I still have places to go, but I want my car. I go straight up to the garage. My baby's there in her usual space, just waiting for me. As I start her up, I notice two shadows break free of the walls in the rearview.

I throw an arm over the seat and turn and look. Bandaged up, both legs jutting forward, Leroy sits in a wheelchair a few short feet from the Benz's rear bumper looking like a reject from an old Lon Chaney mummy picture. He has an angry scowl on his face and a sawed-off shotgun in his hands. Behind him, Ugly, one hand still in a cast, stands holding the now-requisite Glock in the other.

I wonder how the hell he explained himself to Leroy for shooting him.

"Out the car, mufucka! Let's go!"

Unbelievable. I shake my head. Some guys just aren't capable of learning from their mistakes. Maybe that's what Darwin meant about natural selection.

I roll the window down, lean out. "Get out of the way or get mowed down. Your choice, Leroy."

"It's *Leh*-roy, fool. An' I already tol' you—you ain't be givin' me no choices no more. I be givin' you the choices, you got that, bitch?"

I crank the window back up. No time for Leroy tonight. Too much going on. Bigger fish to fry. Discussion over.

"I said you got that?" he shouts, louder now.

I just gun the Benz's engine in response and throw the car into gear. The tires shriek and peel on the floor as I launch the Roadster at them.

Through the rear window, I watch as Leroy's scowl changes from angry to concerned. The shotgun fires. He's too far away to do any real damage, but the window blows in. Glass and shot embed themselves in my face. It hurts—don't think it doesn't—but I've been through worse in the past couple of days. Lots worse.

I keep going.

The more mobile of the two, Ugly manages to dodge out of the way at the last possible second, but Leroy isn't so lucky. He never is. Trapped in the chair, eyes wide and fearful, he tries to wheel out of the way but gets nowhere fast. I plow into him, sending him flying in the cripple chair. He hits a cement pillar and lands with a clatter. Looks painful.

I jam the Benz into drive now. The tires shriek like banshees as I hit the ramp and head down. I don't look back.

24

Reesa's place. Still early. No one home yet. I sit in darkness on her cherry-wood frame futon and smoke and wait. An hour passes and then a key tickles the lock. The door opens. Smelling smoke in the air, Reesa hesitates in the doorway, her figure-eight form backlit by light from the hall.

"Who's there?"

"Just us suckers," I say, as she flips a light on.

"Oh, Mick," she says with a candle flicker smile. She enters a little reluctantly, shuts the door. She doesn't lock it, and I wonder if that's in case she needs to make a quick getaway.

"Aren'tcha happy to see me?"

"W-well of course I am. Of course I am." She slips out of a pair of sandals, comes over and stands in front of me on the pricey oriental carpet. I have to hand it to her, the smile she puts on—the one that says she's glad as hell to see me—is pretty convincing. Up close, she sees the shrapnel damage on my face and switches to a passable look of concern. "Oh baby, what happened to your face?"

"Fender-bender," I say.

"Are you okay?"

"Been better, if you want to know the truth."

She nods. "So, what are you doing here?"

"You told me to come see you when I got out. Or don't you remember that?"

"Sure I do. Sure. I guess I just thought you'd call first."

"I did call. From prison. Thanks for the lawyer by the way."

"I called one. More than one. I just wasn't able to get anybody down there on such short notice. It was pretty late, you know?"

"Late and getting later by the minute."

I drop my cigarette onto the carpet at her feet. I crush it out with the toe of my shoe. I guess I'm feeling a little sore. More than a little. She watches, her happy-to-see-me smile momentarily interrupted by a lightning strike of anger. Then it's back again. Clear skies. That's when I really know it's trouble.

"Is—is something wrong, baby?" she asks.

"You could say that."

"What is it? Tell me."

"Well for starters, on the phone you said I didn't have a motive for killing Callie, except I hadn't told you that was Dallas's real name. For starters."

"You caught that, huh?"

I just nod.

"I guess this must look pretty bad... "

"I guess it must."

"Well, it's not what it looks like."

My turn to smile. "That's the first thing you've said I actually believe," I say. "Because it looks like you hired me to find your sister so you could kill Callie and set me up for it, but that's not it, is it? Otherwise I'd still be in jail."

"That's not it," she agrees quietly.

"Okay, then why don't you tell me what it is?"

"Sure. I'll tell you everything, baby. I was going to anyway, but—it's a long story. You mind if I go slip into something a little more comfortable? Maybe that kimono you like so much, huh?"

"Sure," I say. "No sense being uncomfortable."

Reesa smiles uncertainly and heads for the bedroom. I watch her go. I slow-count to sixty, then I follow her. I find her crouched in her closet, cell phone pressed to her ear. She's surprised to see me. She's even more surprised when I smack the phone out of her hand. It hits the closet wall with a crack.

"Let me guess, you were calling your vampire friend." The statement surprises her. Not because it's wrong, but because it's right and I know it.

"Wh-what are you talking about?"

"Don't play innocent, doll. It doesn't suit ya. If you could act a lick you wouldn't be making a living taking off your clothes. You know exactly what I'm talking about. And who. The blond fella who's been following me around town. Someone altered Tom Kelley's memory, made him forget all about me, and I'm betting it's your friend. Where is he right now? Waiting for me at my place?"

"I don't know what you're—"

She stops short as I raise my hand to hit her. I want to. Despite my rules, despite my past, it takes all my self-control not to do it. Instead, I put murder in my eyes and back her against the hanging clothes.

"Don't you dare touch me," she hisses.

"You didn't seem to mind the other night."

She looks up at me, blinks back hostile tears. "You son-of-a-bitch."

"Better that than being one," I say. "So what's the story? How does a girl like you get herself tangled up with a vampire?"

"You say it like it's a bad thing—"

"It is bad. The worst. If you don't know that, you don't know a goddamn thing."

"Kind of ironic coming from you, don'tcha think?"

My turn to look surprised. Seeing it, Reesa smiles and says, "You think no one knows about you, but people who know *know*."

"They always do."

"So then what's the problem?"

"You don't have to like what you are just because it's what you are."

"I suppose. But you didn't seem to mind when it was you I was tangled up with."

She enjoys throwing the words back in my face. I decide to change the subject. "So how's it work? You go looking for him, or did he come find you?"

"A little of both." She shrugs. "I'd heard rumors about underground vampire covens in L.A. Real ones. I wanted to find out if it was true or not, so I went looking."

I'd heard the same rumors. You don't keep your ear as close to the ground as I do—under it even—and not hear them. But just because you hear a story doesn't make it so. Vampires are an antisocial bunch as a rule. Creating new ones is almost antithetical to the cause. It goes against the basic principles of supply and demand. The more vampires you make, the more competition you have for a dwindling food supply and the better the chance of discovery by said food supply.

"So you went looking and you found a coven?"

"No. But I found Cotney."

"What's a Cotney?"

"My friend. The one who's gonna teach you some manners when he gets here," she smiles, thinking about it before continuing. "He came to my show one night to find out about the girl who was going around asking so many questions about vampires."

"And he agreed to turn you. Just like that."

"No. It took some convincing. And I had to agree to give him something he wanted."

"Your body?"

She smiles cutely. "That too."

"What else?" She looks at me, genuine surprise in her eyes. "You're a lot dumber than I thought. You really don't know? Really?"

When the answer comes it hits me like a medicine ball to the gut. "Your sister."

Reesa nods, her sweet smile as out of place on her face as a money-shot on the Virgin Mary's.

"Why?"

"Why not? I caught the little tramp fucking my boyfriend. I took her in off the street and that's how she repays me?"

"Vin raped her."

"Well, I guess that depends on who you believe."

Discovering that you were right about the world being every bit as fucked up a place as you thought is a small consolation. I feel sick. Sick and disgusted. With her and with me and with everything.

"Where is it?"

She smiles knowingly. "Where's what?"

"The bite mark."

A defiant look on her face, Reesa slowly draws her skirt up a quarter-mile stretch of leg to her waist and shows me two fresh, red and infected-looking puncture marks at the top of her inner thigh, just outside the white silk pouch of her panties.

"You're a goddamn idiot," I tell her.

"You're the idiot," she snaps back. "You're so stupid you're in the middle of all this and you don't know the first thing about what's going on."

"Then educate me. How did Raya end up staying with Callie-Dean?"

"I'd heard about Callie. Word on the street was she knew things. Things about vampires. Things I wanted to know." She shrugs. "She was one of the people I talked to. She's the one who told Cotney about me."

"Yeah? And why were those two so tight?"

"Because Callie-Dean helped Cotney find his victims;

runaways off the street no one would miss. She would go out to clubs and find them. Lure them away from their friends by promising them food and drugs and a free place to crash until Cotney was ready for them."

"Who killed her?"

"Cotney. Who do you think?"

"Why?"

"She was freaked out after you came by. She thought you were on to her. She was sure of it. She was gonna crack. Cotney didn't want that, so… "

There's no need for her to make a gun of one hand and point it at her head, but she does it all the same.

"Well, it all makes perfect sense, except for one little thing," I say.

"What's that?"

"Why did I get dragged into this? Why hire me to find your sister and uncover all this when that's the last thing you should want anyone to know?"

"That's the best part," Reesa says, a sly smile flirting with her lips.

I wait for her to go on. She doesn't.

"What is?" I feel like I'm at the twenty-story top of an amusement park ride in Hell just before the drop.

She shakes her head back and forth. I watch those red curls—the ones I used to like so much—snap like bloody whips about her head.

"You're not gonna tell me?"

More head shakes.

"Why not?"

"It's not my story to tell. It's Cotney's."

"Okay. Why don't you tell me where he is and I'll go ask him."

"I'm right here, hoss."

The Southern accent comes from directly behind me. I know it's blondie without having to look, I can smell his decay, but I turn to look anyway.

Too late. I hear an ominous thwack as something is fired. Then pain—and lots of it—as an object pierces my back and tunnels its way through me to the front. I look down to see the gory tip of what looks to be a wooden crossbow bolt poking out through a ragged hole in my shirt on the left side of my chest. Not good. My whole body goes instantly numb. My knees buckle. Effectively paralyzed, I crumple without feeling to the floor. My head smacks the wood molding of the closet hard. Unable to move, I find myself forced to stare at the pair of two-tone snakeskin cowboy boots directly in front of me.

Cotney kneels down into my field of vision, a mean-looking crossbow in one hand. He's dressed in a pair of worn-out Wranglers and a checked cowboy-cut shirt. His blond hair is longish without being long and pomaded back into a rock-a-billy-style pompadour. His face reminds me of a snub-nosed revolver; a little unfinished and all business. It's a good-looking face, if you don't mind features that look like they might turn mean on a dime.

He flashes his pearly whites my way. "Tell me somethin', hoss, that hurt as much as it looked like it did?"

I try to respond. Try to tell him how if I get the chance I'm

222

going to pull his legs and arms off as if he were a bug, but with the stake in me I only manage a pathetic gurgle.

"What's that? Yer gonna hafta speak up there, pard. Cain't hear ya."

He and Reesa laugh merrily.

"Oh Cotney, you're so bad," Reesa says in a way that makes me wish I'd hit her after all.

Then a hood gets pulled down over my head and the bottom drops out of the world.

25

I have been rolled in a carpet and dumped into the corrugated metal bed of a pickup truck—the '77 Ford is my guess. The engine growls and we head west. I know because I sense the coming sun at our backs. A vampire can always sense the coming sun.

Sea salt stings my nose as we near the Pacific. We hang a right on what must be PCH and head north for Malibu. Or Santa Barbara. Or Canada.

I hear Cotney and Reesa talking together through the sheet metal wall of the cab. It's too faint to make out over the wind and the engine, but I get the gist. She's worried. He reassures her.

We slow. We climb. We twist and turn and stop. Too soon for it to be Canada. Malibu feels about right.

Doors creak open, and then slam. I am picked up again and carried like so much dead meat up a set of stairs and inside, where I am dropped again. Hard. A bolt of pain shreds through me as the wooden shaft in my chest is jostled on landing. I'd scream if I could.

"Sorry 'bout the rough landin' there, hoss," Cotney says, but he doesn't sound sorry. Maybe I'll get the chance to make him that way. Hope so.

Footsteps exit and I'm left alone with only my pain for company.

Cotney's voice rouses me. "Wake up, boy."

I must have blacked out. Opening my eyes, I see I have been unrolled, the hood removed. I find myself propped against a leather couch in a high-ceilinged solarium. In front of me, a wall of windows looks out onto a lighted deck and what must be a spectacular view of a private beach and crashing waves far below.

My gun in hand, Cotney leans cowboy-casual against the sliding glass door, a smile of anticipation on his thin lips. Off to his right, Reesa sits primly on an antique wingback chair. But it is the lithe figure swathed head to toe in black directly in front of me that rivets my attention. I take in the old-fashioned high-necked black lace gown that sweeps down to a pair of gloved hands and polished sharp-toed shoes. An opaque black lace veil hangs from the brim of a lady's black poly-straw hat, obscuring her features. But I don't need to see her face to know her. There's no mistaking the orchids and death scent of her decay. My heart pounds. My stomach drops. A nails-on-chalkboard chill scratches its way down my spine.

Coraline.

"Hello, lover. Surprised to see me?" She goes on without bothering to wait for an answer that won't come anyway. "It was a good try. You only made one little mistake." She shakes a gloved finger and speaks as if to a child. "If you want to kill a vampire you have to scatter the ashes, silly. I mean, if you want to be certain. Otherwise, we can come back."

Good to know. There really should be a goddamn manual.

I try to speak, but nothing comes out.

Coraline looks over at Cotney. "I want to talk to him, darling. Take the stake out, please."

Cotney looks uncertain. "You sure? What if he tries somethin'?"

"If he tries something put a goddamn bullet in his head. You've got the gun, you don't need to be afraid."

Embarrassed, Cotney's eyes jerk tellingly toward Reesa before he can put the brakes on. "I ain't scared a that peckerwood. I ain't scared a no one."

"You forget who you're talking to. I can sense your fear, and frankly, it's an embarrassment."

Cotney goes red as she turns to me and says, "He's nice to look at, but he doesn't have your guts, Mick."

Whether she means it or just wants to humiliate Cotney further, I can't say. Either way, the look of smoldering hatred in his eyes tells me it's not going to turn out good for me. Fuming, he tucks my pistol into the waistband of his Wranglers and stalks over.

"I'll do it gentle, hoss. How'll that be?" he says, going straight to work. He doesn't. What he does is wrench the bolt back and forth like a dog worrying a rope toy, enlarging the already sizable hole in my chest as he jerks it out inch by half-inch. It hurts like hell. I nearly black out again with the pain. Finally, the eight-inch bolt wrenches free with a wet sucking sound and the wall of blackness recedes.

Seeing evidence of all the pain he's inflicted on my face, Cotney grins, dropping the bolt to the floor as he goes back to stand by the sliding glass door.

"That better, lover? Can you talk?"

"Yeah." It comes out as a whisper—barely that. I'm still numb, but now I feel the first sharp pinprick tingles as feeling begins to return.

"Good, because I want to show you what you did to me and hear what you have to say for yourself."

Looking for all the world like a corpse bride on her wedding day, Coraline reaches up and lifts the veil.

From her seat, Reesa is unable to refrain from gasping. I have to agree with her assessment. What lies beneath is worse than anything I could have imagined. I gape at Coraline's ashen skin. It looks stretched and overextended, as if there was not quite enough to go round. Here and there, small moth hole-sized patches are missing, exposing sections of charred bone beneath. Her once near-perfect features appear smeared like melted candle wax across her face. Making it all the more horrible, behind this macabre monster mask I can still just make out the Coraline who used to be. It makes my flesh crawl. There's no hiding the fact. I don't bother to try.

"What's wrong?" Coraline asks bitterly, seeing the look of horror in my eyes. "Don't you like the new me?"

There's nothing there for me. I just turn away.

"Don't you look away from me," Coraline says through clenched teeth. "You did this to me. You look at what you've done, goddamn you."

"You did it to yourself," I tell her, but I don't look. I can't look.

"You know what it was like putting myself back together? You know how awful it was?"

"Well, you did a good job, doll, you should be proud." It's out before I can stop it.

As if waiting for a stage cue, Cotney rushes over and bangs the butt of the gun across my jaw. "You shut yer goddamn mouth! You don't talk to her like 'at."

Stung, Coraline stiffens and drops the veil again, but not before I see venom the likes of which I've never seen flash in her ruined eyes.

"It's okay, dear. If Mick finds the fact that I have to live on forever looking like some kind of circus freak amusing there's nothing we can do about it. It doesn't change anything."

"I hate to point out the obvious, but you weren't actually supposed to live," I say.

"But I did. I did and now you're going to pay for what you've done."

"So that's what all this is about? Revenge?"

"Of course. What else?"

She makes a good point. What else?

"Why'd ya wait so long?"

She tells me how the house burnt and her with it. How it took a long time before she even became aware and even longer before she could come above ground. She tells me about waiting for victims to come along, sometimes for years at a time.

"When I was strong enough I started to plan my revenge. You weren't hard to find. I did a little research and found out you were working as a private investigator." She laughs now, genuinely amused.

"Something funny there?"

"It's just, you're so perfectly cliché, Mick. I mean really, a private dick?"

"It pays the bills."

"Yes, I can see you're doing very well for yourself. Anyway, once I found that out, I thought it would be fun to hire you to find me. I loved the irony of it. So, knowing what a sucker for a damsel in distress you are, I had Cotney find us a girl."

Coraline looks over at Reesa, still seated in the chair. "Lovely, isn't she? Almost as pretty as I was once upon a time, don't you think?"

"Prettier even—"

"You're trying to upset me, but it won't work. I've waited a very long time for my revenge and I'm not going to let you rain on my parade."

"Well, I do love a parade," I say. "One thing I can't figure though—if it's revenge you wanted, why get me out of jail? Why not let me rot?"

"Oh no. That was an accident brought about by Cotney's rash action. Prison is too good for you. I have something much worse in store."

"You wanna let me in on it, or is it gonna be a surprise?"

"It's simple. I'm going to do to you precisely what you did to me. I'm going to put you in a hole in my basement and burn you up and let you slowly piece yourself back together again, because that's all you can do. And decades from now—when you're almost whole—I'm going to burn you all over again. And I'm going to keep on doing it. Forever. So long as we both shall live." The sweet, matter-of-fact way she says it sickens me almost more than the words themselves.

"So that's how it is?"

"That's how it is."

"And what—? You and the hayseed here live happily ever after?"

"Sure. Why not?"

"Pretty idea, but I don't think it's gonna work out that way, baby," I tell her.

"Oh? And why wouldn't it?"

I jerk my head at Reesa. "'Cause your boy—he's in love with her."

"The hell I am," Cotney protests hotly. Too hotly.

I ignore him, all my attention focused on Coraline. "Face it, doll, you've gone and set up a Brasher situation of your very own here. It's only natural a young buck like him is gonna be drawn to someone less—don't take this the wrong way but, well, let's be honest—less monstrous. Way I figure it, it's only a matter of time before you're on your way out. And not a long time either."

"No. You're wrong. He doesn't want her," she says, but she doesn't sound so sure. It's funny how sometimes you're so close to something it takes someone else to point out what you should have seen all along.

"There's a bite mark high on her inner thigh that says different," I say. "See for yourself."

But she doesn't need to see. The twin expressions of guilt and worry on Cotney and Reesa's faces tell her all she needs to know.

"That's what has you so worried," she spits at Cotney. "Not Mick. That he'd say something and I'd find out—"

"No, baby, no. It ain't like that," Cotney says. "This sumbitch is jus' tryin' to make trouble for us. She don't mean nothing to me."

"Then prove it," Coraline says quietly, after a pause. "Shoot her."

All eyes shift to Reesa, who stares back wide-eyed and fearful.

"What?" Cotney smiles a hopeful half-grin like maybe it's all a joke and he's ready to laugh along.

"You heard me. Put a bullet in her pretty little head and then set her on fire. Let's let Mick see what's in store for him."

"No. You can't—" Reesa says, the skin of her face pulled tight. "I did everything you wanted. I gave you my sister. I helped you get him." She nods at me, frantic.

"And sniffing around my man like a bitch in heat—you think I wanted that?"

"No. I—I wasn't trying—It wasn't like that." Tears welling, Reesa turns to Cotney and pleads. "Cotney, tell her it wasn't like that."

"Baby, she's right. It wasn't."

"I'm not going to argue with you. I told you to shoot her.

Now do it." Coraline's voice is terminally cold. If Cotney knows her at all, he knows there is no more room for argument when she sounds that way.

He knows. The gun floats from me to Reesa like driftwood on an outgoing tide. When it stops, he seems almost as surprised to see it pointing at her as she is.

Rather than move away, Reesa lurches toward him and drops to her knees and clutches him hard around the legs, all pretenses gone now. "Cotney. Cotney, you can't do this. You said everything would be okay. You said we'd be together forever. You promised me, Cotney."

Biting his lip, Cotney gently places the gun barrel dead center on her forehead. Her wet, red eyes plead up at him. She shakes her head, no, once. It is a small thing and there is no defiance in it.

A long moment passes. Cotney's finger tightens on the trigger, and I think that's all for Reesa, but at the last possible second, he spins and points the gun at Coraline instead.

"I love her," he says with a sheepish smile, and pulls the trigger over and over.

He's a good shot, even with a snub-nose. A nice grouping of bullets slam home in the black lace covering Coraline's chest. Some exit out her back. Some don't. Stunned at this development, Coraline falls to the floor, sucking wetly for breath through shredded lungs.

I take the opportunity to make my move. Transforming as I go, I grab the crossbow bolt from the carpet and lunge for Cotney. Seeing me coming, he manages to get a bullet in my gut as he too metamorphoses.

It hurts, but it doesn't stop me. Doesn't even slow me down. When I reach him, my momentum sends us crashing through the sliding glass door behind him and we land on the deck beyond, snapping and clawing like a pair of rabid dogs. I knock the gun from his hand and attempt to jam the stake into him, but he catches me by the wrist. With his free hand he grabs me by the hair and attempts to pull me within reach of those lethal fangs.

Maybe it's because I haven't fed enough today. Maybe it's the gaping hole in my chest. Maybe it's the fresh bullet wound. Whatever the case, Cotney manages to hold the stake at bay while pulling me close enough to get his mouth on me. I feel his breath on my neck and then his teeth sink home and he begins to drink me dead.

My head spins. Knowing time is short, I dig in with my feet and heave with my legs in a final desperate lunge. It's enough. I drive the stake into his heart. The drinking stops. Because he is immobilized I actually have to use my hands to free my neck from those bear-trap jaws.

"You wanted to know how it felt. Now you know," I say, changing back to human form.

Exhausted, I push back and get to my knees as the business end of the .38 presses to my head. It's no surprise to find Reesa at the other end. She doesn't say a word. Just pulls the trigger.

Click. Empty. Too bad for her the last bullet is already in me.

Her eyes go wide as she realizes her predicament. I stand slowly, testing my limbs. Everything hurts.

Terrified, she drops the gun and flees down the long flight of wooden stairs to the moonlit beach below.

I watch her go. Then I break a slat from the wooden deck fence and head back inside, dragging Cotney by the hair behind me. The expression in his eyes seems to suggest he can't believe it's come to this. I guess that's how everyone feels when the end comes sooner than expected.

I find Coraline still hacking and wheezing where she fell. Looks painful. I kneel by her and remove her hat and veil. I stare down into her melty eyes. I can't tell if it's love or hate I see there. Maybe it's all the same thing to a woman like Coraline.

As I center the crude stake over her heart, she reaches up and takes hold of my wrist weakly. "Do me a favor and scatter the ashes this time, lover," she says in a waning whisper. "I don't want to come back like this."

I nod once. Then I drive the stake down. Hard.

26

I follow Reesa up the beach. It's a simple matter, just follow the tracks in the sand. I can see her up ahead running along the water's edge, skirt held high to keep it from tripping her. Her hair looks like spun blood in the moonlight; so lovely it makes me salivate.

She screams when my hand falls on her neck. She never heard me coming. She turns and fights. Her fists beat at my face and chest until I grab them and make them stop. She struggles a moment more and then the fight goes out of her.

"Kill me. I don't care. I'll just become what I want to be anyway. Like you."

I stare down into her defiant eyes. I don't hunt women. I don't feed on them. I don't hurt them. No women, no children, no innocents, those are the rules. My rules. Without them I become what I dread most—a monster.

But this one—she's no innocent. She's already infected. The disease is in her. So the question becomes, when is a vampire truly a vampire? Maybe it's as futile as trying to determine when a fetus becomes a baby, but someone has to decide, don't they? Someone has to take responsibility, because maybe sometimes an abortion is necessary. If you knew, really knew, that the kid was going to grow up to be a Hitler, or a Bundy— or Coraline, for instance. Maybe that makes bending a rule all right. Breaking it even.

I look at her. I give her the gaze. "Let's go back to the house," I say.

The fear and defiance ebb from her eyes, leaving a vacancy sign behind.

"Back," she murmurs.

The moonlight shimmers on the wet sand like a chalk outline around a body. We retrace our steps to the beach house hand in hand. Anyone seeing us now would just think we were lovers out for a romantic late night stroll.

We leave the sand behind for weathered wood and creaking stairs. We go up and in.

"Lay down and close your eyes," I say gently.

The sun is coming. I feel its approach like a fever. Have to hurry now.

Reesa goes over to her oriental carpet and lies down and closes her eyes just as I've told her. Watching her, my conscience tugs at me, but having a conscience doesn't mean you can't go against it now and then. It just means maybe you won't like yourself much in the morning if you do.

So there it is.

I bend and kiss those perfect lips. Then I stand and light a smoke and wonder how the hell I'm going to make myself do what I know needs doing...

In the end it's as simple as dropping a match.

A NOTE FROM THE AUTHOR

I came up with the idea for *Angel of Vengeance* and the character Mick Angel sometime in 2005. At that point, I had already had a long love affair with vampires, but I'd never written anything in the genre. To me it was only a worthwhile pursuit if I had a new and fresh way in to the vampire mythos. The idea for a hard-boiled, noir vampire story came to me after rereading *Dracula* and following it up with a Raymond Chandler novel. Blending two of the genres I loved best by creating a blood-sucking Phillip Marlowe who was turned in the forties, and continued on as a living anachronism in the present day seemed like it held a lot of potential to be that story.

The novel that resulted is a much darker tale than that depicted in *Moonlight*, the TV show that eventually evolved from it. Having gone down a promising, but ultimately dead-end road with a previous unpublished crime novel, I decided the best route to publication was to return to my Hollywood roots by adapting the manuscript into a feature screenplay, and work backwards to publishing the novel. The result was that I ended up being put together with Ron Koslow (creator of *Beauty and the Beast*, and a man I have come to consider a good friend and mentor) to create a pilot for CBS for the 2006 development season.

What Ron and I came up with was, in many ways, a lighter, more romantic version of the dark noir Los Angeles underbelly I had created in the book, but it retained many of the novel's themes of redemption and transcendence. The mandate from CBS was that they loved the main character and the vampire world, but they wanted the show to have a strong romantic angle. As a result, one of the first challenges Ron and I faced was to find a romantic core for the story to revolve around. We decided that Coraline was far too dark and dangerous a femme fatale to be Mick's constant love interest. As a potential solution, I mentioned to Ron that although there was no Mick/Beth romance in my first novel, Mick does save a little girl from Coraline, and I had been thinking of exploring the ensuing romance between Mick and the grown up girl he watches over in a later novel, which I planned to call "Guardian Angel". He liked the idea. With Ron on board, the concept for *Moonlight* was born, and together he and I hashed out a new mythology for the characters that would come to populate the series. A whirlwind year and a half later, despite having built a strong and rabid fan-base, and winning the People's Choice Award for best new drama, the show had sadly come and gone, and I had yet to find a publisher for the novel that spawned it.

For a while, it looked as if the window was gone, and that perhaps the book would never be published at all. But much like vampires themselves, a good vampire story dies hard, and in the past year, with the help of those who continued to believe in it, the manuscript found its way into the hands of the good people at Titan who offered to publish it. As a result, my long-term plan to work backwards to the novel has finally come to be. I hope you have enjoyed the read as much as I enjoyed the writing of it. It was truly a labor of love and love lost for me.

T.O.M., October 2010

ABOUT THE AUTHOR

Photograph by Marc Blackwell

Trevor Munson began his Hollywood career when his script 'Lone Star State of Mind' was bought and produced in 2002 by Sony Screen Gems. Trevor went on to write his first novel, *Angel of Vengeance*, which eventually became the CBS television series *Moonlight* for which he was Co-Creator and Co-Executive Producer.

ACKNOWLEDGMENTS

Thanks to everyone who helped make this novel a reality, from those who read it and didn't hate it in its early stages, to those who believed in it when no one else did. I couldn't have done it without you. As those who know, know, the road to publication for this novel was a long and arduous one. Special thanks to my manager, Kevin Donahue, who always believed and was a driving force in finding others who did too. Also, sincere thanks to my WME literary agent, Rebecca Oliver, and my Titan editor, Jo Boylett, for shepherding the project and helping me hone it for human consumption. A six year-old boy with an idea of somehow becoming an author one day thanks you for helping him realize his dream…

AVAILABLE MAY 2011

ANNO DRACULA
Kim Newman

It is 1888 and Dracula has married Queen Victoria
and turned a large percentage of the English population
into undead.

Peppered with familiar characters from Victorian
history and fiction — Dr Jekyll, Oscar Wilde,
Swinburne, John Jago — the story follows vampire
Genevieve Dieudonné and human Charles Beauregard
of the Diogenes Club as they strive to solve the mystery
of the Ripper murders.

ISBN: 9780857680839

WWW.TITANBOOKS.COM

OUT NOW

SUPERNATURAL: HEART OF THE DRAGON
Keith R.A. DeCandido

The brothers face the powerful spirit behind a series of
particularly brutal killings in San Francisco's Japantown.

ISBN: 9781848566002

SUPERNATURAL: THE UNHOLY CAUSE
Joe Schreiber

When a Civil War reenactment in Georgia becomes all too
real, Sam and Dean head south to investigate.

ISBN: 9781848565289

SUPERNATURAL: WAR OF THE SONS
Rebecca Dessertine & David Reed

The boys find themselves in a small town in South Dakota
where they meet an angel with a proposition.

ISBN: 9781848566019

COMING SOON

SUPERNATURAL: ONE YEAR GONE
Rebecca Dessertine

Dean travels to Salem in search of a way to resurrect Sam,
but his brother is not as far away as he thinks.

ISBN: 9780857680990

SUPERNATURAL: COYOTE'S KISS
Christa Faust

Sam and Dean discover murder and a whole new
world of monsters at the Mexican border.

ISBN: 9780857681003

WWW.TITANBOOKS.COM

THE FURTHER ADVENTURES OF SHERLOCK HOLMES SERIES

OUT NOW

THE VEILED DETECTIVE David Stuart Davies
ISBN: 9781848564909

THE WAR OF THE WORLDS
Manly Wade Wellman & Wade Wellman
ISBN: 9781848564916

THE ECTOPLASMIC MAN Daniel Stashower
ISBN: 9781848564923

THE SCROLL OF THE DEAD David Stuart Davies
ISBN: 9781848564930

THE MAN FROM HELL Barrie Roberts
ISBN: 9781848565081

THE STALWART COMPANIONS H. Paul Jeffers
ISBN: 9781848565098

THE SEVENTH BULLET Daniel D. Victor
ISBN: 9781848566767

SÉANCE FOR A VAMPIRE Fred Saberhagen
ISBN: 9781848566774

DR JEKYLL AND MR HOLMES Loren D. Estleman
ISBN: 9781848567474

THE WHITECHAPEL HORRORS Edward B. Hanna
ISBN: 9781848567498

THE GIANT RAT OF SUMATRA Richard L. Boyer
ISBN: 9781848568600

THE ANGEL OF THE OPERA Sam Siciliano
ISBN: 9781848568617

COMING SOON

THE PEERLESS PEER Philip José Farmer
ISBN: 9780857681201

THE STAR OF INDIA Carole Buggé
ISBN: 9780857681218

WWW.TITANBOOKS.COM

OUT NOW

RUNESCAPE

BETRAYAL AT FALADOR
T.S. Church

In the kingdom of Asgarnia, the Knights of Falador
defend the land and protect the people. But when
a young woman's stormy arrival launches a chain
of events that endangers the very fabric of magic,
the knights must solve the riddle of Kara-Meir or
everything they hold close may be lost. But hope may
lie with an untested squire named Theodore.

ISBN: 9781848567221

RETURN TO CANIFIS
T.S. Church

In Varrock, the greatest human city in the world, people
are being taken by an inhuman abductor, its victims
murdered... or worse, spirited away to Morytania,
where vampires rule. As unrest grows, the King sends
the now-famous Kara-Meir and her friends across the
holy river into Morytania, the land of the dead.

ISBN: 9781848567276

WWW.TITANBOOKS.COM